'I don't remember you getting the blanket last night?'

'It got a little cold around three o'clock.' He'd woken to find her shivering a little in his arms, and although their bodies had provided quite a lot of heat, it hadn't been enough. So he'd carefully removed her, sorted out the blanket, and repositioned himself, happily gathering Chloe back into his arms.

He'd been glad she'd slept through, and while he'd been holding her, listening to her steady breathing, he'd placed a kiss to the top of her head, amazed at how right she'd seemed to feel in his arms. He'd felt it before, when they'd jumped from the plane, but this had been different. Simply holding her had given him such calm pleasure and quiet satisfaction. And he hadn't experienced those emotions in a very long time.

GW00362189

Lucy Clark began writing romance in her early teens, and immediately knew she'd found her 'calling' in life. After working as a secretary in a busy teaching hospital, she turned her hand to writing medical romance. She currently lives in South Australia, with her husband and two children. Lucy largely credits her writing success to the support of her husband, family and friends.

Recent titles by the same author:

IN HIS SPECIAL CARE
A KNIGHT TO HOLD ON TO
CHRISTMAS DAY FIANCÉE*
CRISIS AT KATOOMBA HOSPITAL*
DR CUSACK'S SECRET SON

Blue Mountains A&E

THE SURGEON'S COURAGEOUS BRIDE

BY
LUCY CLARK

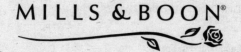

MILLS & BOON®

All the characters in this book have no existence outside the imagination of the author, and have no relation whatsoever to anyone bearing the same name or names. They are not even distantly inspired by any individual known or unknown to the author, and all the incidents are pure invention.

First published in Great Britain 2006
Paperback edition 2007
Harlequin Mills & Boon Limited,
Eton House, 18-24 Paradise Road, Richmond, Surrey TW9 1SR

© Lucy Clark 2006

ISBN-13: 978 0 263 85217 2
ISBN-10:   0 263 85217 2

Set in Times Roman 10½ on 12½ pt
03-0107-48370

Printed and bound in Spain
by Litografia Rosés, S.A., Barcelona

THE SURGEON'S COURAGEOUS BRIDE

To Kerryn & David,
who have found their happily ever after.
Congratulations.
1 Cor 13

medical training had taught him to remain calm in all situations but this was one situation they hadn't covered in lectures or textbooks.

'Strap in,' Chloe called, and Michael hefted himself over to his seat, strapped himself in and crossed his arms, resting them on the seat in front of him.

His heart was pounding fiercely against his chest. Well, he'd wanted to feel alive, and right now he'd never felt more alive in his life. Strange. He felt the most alive just before he was about to die.

CHAPTER TWO

MICHAEL opened his eyes, feeling the pain in his head. He lay still, the sound of his heart reverberating in his ears. He looked around, taking in the situation, his brain working overtime as he figured out where he was. Things were a little blurry and he squinted, trying to focus on what was around him. No good. He couldn't see much. He closed his eyes and waited for his mind to clear.

He searched for his last known memory, going through the usual things. His name was Michael Hill. He was a general surgeon. He worked at Sydney General hospital three days a week and two days at a private practice. He drove a green Jaguar, his current pride and joy, which he liked to drive fast. He could count to twenty and remembered his alphabet.

Had he been involved in a car accident? Perhaps. He tried to move and found himself restrained. Seat belt? He carefully felt his body but only found the lap-sash. Not in a car. He opened his eyes again, this time able to focus more clearly…even though it was quite dark. He was on a plane. Why was he on a plane?

One flash after another started shooting through his

mind as he recalled accepting the job with PMA to fly to Tarparnii and retrieve a sick VIP. Then the memories came. The noise of the stressed plane engines, the violent shaking and the smell of one hundred per cent fear as the plane had crashed.

He tested his limbs and found everything in working order. There seemed to be a glimmer of light somewhere to his left and he slowly turned his head in that direction. The plane appeared to be tipped at a ten-degree angle to the right.

Michael needed to get out of his seat, to check on his patient as well as the other passengers. He hoped that Chloe was all right, as he'd probably need her help to get the situation under control. He tried to undo his seat belt but found it jammed. It didn't seem to matter how hard he pressed the button and wriggled, the buckle was stuck fast. He tried the belt where it was secured to the frame of the seat but found it just as secure.

'This is good. It's good to know the seat belt works, that it keeps me safe and probably saved my life… somehow.' He gazed down at the inanimate object. 'But you can let me go now,' he all but yelled.

'Hey.'

Michael froze at the sound of another voice and turned his head to try and look over his shoulder. 'Chloe?'

'Who else would it be?' she replied. 'Can you move?'

Michael tugged at the belt again to no avail. 'You're all right?' He was surprised to feel happiness at the thought, although he had no idea why. He didn't even know the woman but, given what they'd just been through, having someone else alive was a good thing.

'Bruised and battered but otherwise OK. What's wrong with you?'

'Seat belt is jammed.'

At his words, she shone the beam from her medical torch down to where the seat belt was attached. She shifted closer to him and he could see she had scratches on her face, blood oozing slowly from a gash above her right eyebrow.

'You're hurt.'

Chloe waved away his concern. 'Just a scratch. I've had worse. How about you? Anything broken?'

'No.' He paused, breathing in her floral scent, and this time he found it mildly comforting. Usually that scent dredged up memories of his ex-girlfriend—the only woman who had even come close to getting him to think about walking down the aisle. 'I've seen worse, too.'

'Good. Means you're a survivor.'

The woman had no idea just how right she was.

'You're obviously stuck,' she said. 'Let's see what I can do about that.'

Michael shifted in his seat again, beginning to get annoyed at the inconvenience of being unable to move.

'Sit still.' Her tone was stern. She leaned closer again, tendrils of her blonde hair brushing his cheek as she leaned over. Michael was mesmerised at how close she was, how incredible she smelt and how wonderful her hair felt as it tickled his skin. Her gaze flicked up, just for a second, and met his. In that one instant he realised he wouldn't mind kissing her, discovering the feel of her lips against his. Ludicrous. That's what it was.

She looked away, moving her head down so he couldn't see her face. Was she embarrassed? His intrigue grew. He'd felt instant attraction before but hadn't always pursued it, and he realised this would be one of those occasions where things were best left alone. They both had a job to do and the job came first.

Focus, Chloe, she told herself. She'd never found it this difficult in the past to concentrate on her job. Then again, she'd never been involved in a plane crash or met a man like Michael Hill before. It was ridiculous and she knew she'd probably been mistaken, but had his blue gaze just encompassed her as though he'd wanted to kiss her? No. She must be mistaken.

Chloe knew she was average-looking and that on the odd occasion in the past men had found her attractive, but not here, not now. Yet the look in her new colleague's eyes had honestly made her feel as though she was both perfect and desirable. True, the look had been fleeting and, no doubt, she'd misinterpreted the signals. It had been a very long time since she'd had to read a man's body language as far as personal interest was concerned. Then again, why was she even thinking about it now? She wasn't interested in any relationships other than working ones. Surviving had been her goal for the past six years and now it appeared surviving a plane crash was her top priority.

'Wait there.'

'Where am I going to go?' he asked, then muttered something about dumb-fool questions. Chloe couldn't help the smile that touched her lips at his retort. She unlatched a locker and pulled out a sterile scalpel, ripping it from its cover.

'Hold still.' She sliced through the seat belt and tried not to smile at the sight he made as he slumped into the bulkhead.

'A little warning would have been nice,' he muttered.

'And miss the surprised look on your face?'

Michael shifted to look at her, pleased and intrigued to find the teasing edge of her personality. It appeared there was more to Chloe than first met the eye.

'You think I'm surprised?' He shook his head and rubbed his neck when it jarred. 'That wouldn't have been the adjective I'd have chosen.' Michael tried to stand but found his legs tingling with pins and needles.

'Take it easy,' Chloe insisted. 'You're like a foal trying to stand for the first time.'

'Nice analogy.' He shifted again but more slowly this time. 'How's the patient?'

'Don't know.' She watched him stand. 'You all right?'

'Yes.' His tone was back to being clipped, the same as when she'd boarded.

She turned her back and stumbled over to the lockers before reaching for the emergency torches. 'Here.' She handed one to him. 'Check on the General and I'll see if his wife is all right.'

He nodded and pulled himself up, climbing across the seat and making his way to the General's side. 'Harleem?' he called, but received no response. 'General?' With the tilt of the plane, it made standing difficult but also gave him a bit more head room. Always find the positive. It was what his parents had drummed into him from an early age, although there had been many times when the positive had been difficult to find. He grimaced, wondering if that was the only one he was going to find in this disastrous situation.

He checked the General, glad to find the straps had held the patient secure. He pressed two fingers to

Harleem's carotid pulse, relieved to feel it was still there. Unlatching one of the lockers, trying not to let other things spill out, he pulled out a stethoscope.

'The wife is breathing but unconscious,' Chloe announced. 'Minor cuts and bruises. I'm going to leave her where she is for now and check on the pilots.' She cleared her throat, then said in a more sombre tone, 'And the bodyguard is dead.'

The bodyguard! Michael had temporarily forgotten about him. He shone his torch around the plane to where the large Tarparniian man was slumped sideways in his seat, his neck at an odd angle.

Chloe swallowed. 'His neck's broken.' She glanced at Michael. 'Let's focus on what we can do to help.'

'Right.' He positioned his torch under his left armpit, trying to shed light on the General before hooking the stethoscope into place and listening to Harleem's chest. He was pleased to hear everything was normal…or as normal as it could be in such circumstances. He still felt as though he were in some sort of nightmare. Crashing in a jungle? A sabotaged plane? What kind of life was this he'd fallen into?

One he'd wanted, came the answer. He'd tried a lot of foolish things during the past four years, but this surely took the prize. He'd tried sky-diving, sky-boarding, rock-climbing, abseiling and many other fairly extreme sports. Although they all had their inherent risks, they'd been risks he'd accepted with every effort made to ensure safety. When he'd joined PMA—this retrieval being a sort of trial—he'd expected adventure and the need for improvised medicine, but surviving a plane crash in the middle of a hostile environment was more than he'd bargained for.

He shook his head to clear his thoughts and started doing the neurological observations. Chloe was right. They needed to help where they could and his primary focus was making sure his VIP patient made it through this ordeal.

'How is he, Michael?' Chloe asked from the entrance to the cockpit.

'Stable. I'll need to monitor him closely.'

She nodded. 'Can you come take a look at the pilots, please?' Without waiting for an answer, she disappeared back the way she'd come.

'You wanted adventure,' he mumbled, as he grabbed his stethoscope and torch, before rummaging in a few of the lockers that weren't jammed, finding bandages and pain relievers. His hands full, he picked his way carefully through the debris of the plane.

'Look at Smith first,' Chloe announced as soon as she heard Michael. Her tone was matter-of-fact and direct yet Michael detected a hint despair. She squeezed out of the way to allow him into the small space. Michael simply stood there and stared at the sight before him, lit by both their torches. The nose of the plane had been badly compressed and twisted, the front windscreen broken and smashed, bits of leaves and branches poking through. One tree branch, a thick one, had impaled Smith in the abdomen.

'He's unconscious.' Chloe pressed two fingers to Smith's carotid pulse. 'At least that's something,' she said softly. Michael crouched down and pulled on a pair of gloves he'd found.

'Hi, there,' he said to Smith. 'I'm Michael. Can you hear me?' He checked Smith's pupils and found them sluggish. 'I need more light,' he commanded and in the next instant Chloe was shining the light from a powerful torch she'd found in the cockpit. The tree branch had done a good job, going diagonally through the abdomen, but didn't appear to have gone right through.

'It's not good.'

'No,' she agreed.

'Let me look at the other one.'

'But Smith is in a worse condition.'

'And one I can do nothing for.'

'But we have to help him,' Chloe insisted.

'Then give him something for the pain.'

'But—'

'His injuries are too extensive.' Michael's words were firm and he shifted around to face the co-pilot. The man started groaning, regaining consciousness, which was a good sign. Chloe disappeared and he knew she was cross with him, but that was her problem.

'Hi, I'm Michael,' he said to the co-pilot. 'What's your name?'

'Gary.'

'Hi, Gary. Remember where you are?'

'In a plane. Where else would I be?'

'Of course. Do you remember what happened?'

'We crashed in the jungle. We're in Tarparn—' He winced in pain.

'Where does it hurt the most?' Michael asked.

'Legs.'

Michael shone the torch down at Gary's legs. The metal of the plane was twisted around them. Terrific. Now they had three critically injured patients, although he seriously doubted whether Smith would make it.

Right now he needed more supplies. He needed more hands, more staff. He needed the equipment of a well-stocked A and E department and, while he was wishing, a bit more light wouldn't go astray. Instead, he was in a crashed plane, in the middle of a jungle, in a country in the midst of civil unrest—at night!

'How's Smithy doing?' West asked.

'Let's just concentrate on you. Can you describe exactly where the pain is? Upper part of the leg? Lower? Just your toes?'

Gary thought for a moment. 'Can't feel my toes. I might be wiggling them but I can't tell.'

'Hey, look who's woken up.' Chloe came back into the small space, holding supplies. She put them down and pulled on a pair of gloves. 'Nice to have you back with us, West.'

West forced a smile. 'Glad to have you both on board. Don't worry about me. Look after Smithy.'

'Chloe'll take care of him,' said Michael gently, as he checked West's pupils. 'Let's get a drip set up for you and some analgesics.' He glanced over his shoulder to where Chloe was drawing up an injection. Her face was devoid of emotion but her body language said she was cross with him. Well, that was just too bad. They were in a tight situation and he wasn't about to waste precious medical resources on a patient who would soon die. That might seem cold and uncaring but he was only thinking ahead. Who knew how long they'd be in this plane or what would happen to them?

He reached for the bag of saline and tubing she'd brought in and looked around for somewhere to hang the bag. He shone his torch and found a lever just to the rear of the cockpit bulkhead. He hung the bag up and connected the rest of it. Chloe handed him a pair of heavy-duty scissors.

'Thanks.'

'Hmm,' was all she said, and he nodded, now positive she was cross with him.

He cut West's sleeve off his shirt, pulling it away in order to find a good vein. Chloe thankfully provided him with light and soon the drip was operational, complete with painkillers.

'You do his obs, I'll provide the light,' Michael said, needing to stretch from his cramped confines.

'Fine.' The word was clipped but she manoeuvred herself in and began to examine the pilot. Gary appeared able to move his entire body, except his legs.

'Actually, I can kind of feel my right leg but nothing on my left.'

Chloe nodded. 'But you can move your arms all right?'

'Yes.'

'OK.' She made mental notes of everything, wishing she had charts on which to write everything down. She sighed. 'We'll go from there.'

'Shh,' West said suddenly.

'What is it?' Chloe asked.

'Shh.' West held up a hand. Everyone was silent. 'Pass me the torch.' She did so and West shone the light onto the panel of instruments in front of him. 'Er... slight problem.'

Michael felt another wave of apprehension and fear grip him at the co-pilot's tone but he focused on what he was doing.

'The starboard fuel tank.' West gestured with his

hand towards the instruments he was talking about. 'The gauge is dropping.'

'We're leaking fuel?' Chloe's words were hollow.

'I thought I could smell something. Switch off the electrics.' Again West pointed to what he needed her to do. 'The tiniest spark and we're all charcoal.'

'Just what we really don't need.' She did as she was told. 'Should I take a look?'

'Someone should. If it's just dripping to the ground and nothing's around to spark it, we should be fine.' West handed the torch back to Chloe.

She turned and looked at Michael, who was kneeling down so he could stretch his arms. They were above his head, his trousers dipping and his shirt riding up to reveal a tiny hint of his flat, muscled stomach. Chloe's eyes widened and for a second she was unable to look away. It had been a long time…a *very* long time…since she'd seen a male body this close. Oh, she wasn't talking about patients, they didn't count. She'd worked with many male colleagues over the years and even in Tarparnii, despite the heat, they all kept their shirts on. Or at least she'd never been affected by one in this way before.

Unconsciously, she raised a hand to her cheek, finding it warm. Goodness. She was blushing! She looked away, using the darkness as a shield. Had Michael seen? Seen her looking at him? Seen her reaction? Oh, this wasn't good. She'd been about to say something to him but for the life of her she couldn't remember what. It was wrong. She always remembered, she never lost focus, yet in the few hours since she'd met Michael Hill she'd lost focus several times, which was ridiculous because the man meant nothing to her. Absolutely nothing.

'I'll go.' Michael's deep voice broke into her thoughts.

'No. It's fine. I can do it,' she snapped, needing to get away from him, to get some air. To try and pull herself together. 'You need to check on the General.' She retied her ponytail and briefly met his gaze.

As before, there were undercurrents flowing between the two of them. Earlier, when she'd been trying to free him from his seat belt, she'd felt exactly the same sensation as now. It was one where she wanted to be held against his body, to have his arms come around hers to assure her they would be all right. Was that all? Was that all she wanted from him? Comfort? Reassurance? No. She also knew that she wanted to know what it was like to have his mouth pressed to hers, and that thought in itself told her just how crazily she was behaving. She didn't even *like* Michael.

'I'll just stay here,' West said, thankfully breaking the moment between them.

'Right.' Michael turned away and made his way back through the plane to the General. What had that been? Another acknowledgement that he found Chloe... He couldn't even remember her last name and yet he found her attractive. Even when she was mad with him. 'Ridiculous,' he muttered as reached the General's side.

Michael was reluctantly impressed by her, though he struggled not to be. She was beautiful, smart and clearly brave. He liked a woman who wasn't afraid to stand up, not only for herself but for the things she believed in. He also liked a woman who would pitch in and get her hands dirty if necessary and there Chloe was, fulfilling every requirement on his check list.

But right now he didn't need to think about the

blonde doctor. Their situation was at best dire. They had one dead passenger, one pilot who wouldn't make it through the next hour, a man whose leg looked as though it was welded to the plane, a VIP requiring emergency surgery and an unconscious wife. Sexual attraction to a colleague was something he could do without. Besides, could things get any worse?

At that moment, he heard a loud rumble…a rumble of thunder.

'Obviously.' The word was said without enthusiasm and with a large serving of dread.

Chloe entered the cabin and he found he was conscious of her movements without even looking at her.

'The wife is still unconscious,' she reported.

'Probably for the best at the moment.'

'How's the General?'

'Stable, for now.'

'I'm going to head out and take a look around.' She moved to the door but after three attempts couldn't budge it.

Without being asked, Michael crossed to her side and put his hand on the door at the exact moment she did, and for a moment her hand was on top of his. A flare of tingles spread up her arm and exploded throughout her body. What on earth was happening between them? Was it just the situation they were in? Yes. That had to be it. Their senses were heightened due to the danger they were facing. That was a logical and rational explanation. She quickly removed her hand.

'Will you be all right?' he asked as he heaved on the doorhandle, managing to move it.

'Sure.'

'Do you want me to go out with you?'

'I'll only be outside.' She paused. 'Although I thought I might try and have a look around, see where we are.'

'You'd be better off doing that when there's a bit more natural light.'

'Good point. Right. I'll go check this fuel leak.'

'You've got a torch?'

'Yes.' She flicked it on as he lowered the door, the steps not reaching the ground. He found himself holding her arm as she stepped tentatively onto the first step. 'I'll be fine,' she said, and looked pointedly down to where he was touching her. He instantly let go.

'Call if you need any help.'

'Will do.' With that, she jumped the space between the last step and the ground. As she disappeared into the darkness, Michael felt a thread of concern push through him.

'Ridiculous,' he said, and tried to move away from the door, but found he couldn't.

CHAPTER THREE

THE thunder continued to rumble its way towards them and ten minutes later Chloe still hadn't returned. What was she doing? She was only supposed to check a fuel leak. Couldn't she find it? He shook his head, knowing he should have insisted he go. Did she even know what she was looking for?

It had taken him a whole three minutes to move from the doorway but he still kept a close ear out for strange sounds. Nothing came. The General moaned in pain and he crossed to the man's side to examine him. He shook his head. Things were getting worse.

A moment later he heard a noise and crossed back to the doorway, shining his torch to provide extra light. He felt rather than saw Chloe step onto the lower step and in another second she was inside the plane.

'What took you so long?' Michael demanded.

'Huh?' She frowned at his unexpected attack.

'You only had to go and check a fuel leak. That's all. That doesn't take over ten minutes, Chloe.'

'Well, it did this time,' she retorted, as she pushed past him, totally annoyed with his attitude.

'Do you even know what you were supposed to be looking for?'

She stopped at his words and turned slowly to face him, her hands planted on her hips. He could see in the beam of his torch that she was angry. If that hadn't given him a clue to her mood, the way she spoke so soft and precisely did. 'I beg your pardon?' She paused, waiting for him to speak, but instead Michael just stood there. 'I knew exactly what I was looking for, thank you very much. My father is a mechanic who deemed it necessary for me to not only know my way around the inner workings of a car but any other piece of machinery. Next time I'll thank you to keep your chauvinistic comments to yourself.'

And that put him firmly in his place, he realised as she shuffled her way through to the cockpit, stopping to check on the wife *en route*. Michael watched her go and realised the error he'd made. Not only had he made her mad with his comments, which, he realised, probably did come across as though he were a card-carrying member of the chauvinists' club, but he'd discovered that when she was angry, her brown eyes became the colour of deep, rich chocolate. Of course, he couldn't be one hundred per cent sure due to the lack of natural light, but he wouldn't mind making her mad when daybreak came, just to be certain.

He returned to the General's side. Oh, yes, Chloe… whatever her surname was was turning out to be quite the little spitfire.

Michael checked the General again and where before he'd thought things had been starting to get worse, he now knew they were. He slipped the blood-pressure cuff around Harleem's arm and pumped it up, not liking the reading he received when he'd finished. The General's blood pressure was dropping. He checked the drip, wondering if there was a blockage somewhere, but it was working perfectly.

He checked the Harleem's pupils. Still fine. He listened to his chest. Fine. He took a blood-pressure reading again. Still dropping. He slowly began to remove the padded bandages around the General's abdomen.

Michael noted a fresh, brighter red stain and realised the General had an internal bleed somewhere. He shook his head, knowing he needed to find the offending arteries and suture them off.

'Chloe?' he called loudly.

'You yelled?' she said a moment later as she stood in the doorway to the cockpit.

'I need you. The General's bleeding somewhere. His BP is dropping.'

Chloe instantly made her way through the plane, becoming expert at precisely where to put her feet. As she passed the General's wife, she felt a cool hand grab her arm, and she gasped in surprise before realising the other woman had finally regained consciousness.

'It's all right,' Chloe reassured her in Tarparnese. 'You're OK.'

The woman grabbed frantically at Chloe's arm, tears in her eyes. 'Where am I?' she whispered.

'Chloe?' Michael called impatiently.

Chloe clenched her teeth and turned back to the woman. 'You were in a plane crash. What's your name?'

'Kirsa.' She paused. 'Harleem?'

'I need to see to him now. The doctor and I need to

fix Harleem to make him better.' Chloe tried to move but Kirsa still held her arm.

'He will live?'

'I need to see him *now.*' She removed Kirsa's hand and patted it reassuringly. 'Stay there. I'll look at you when I can.'

'What are you doing?' Michael called as he lifted the bloodstained bandage from Harleem's abdomen. 'I need more bandages.'

'I'm coming.' She quickly crossed to the lockers and opened the one that contained the bandages. She ripped open the sterile dressing and held it out to Michael. He grabbed it, as well as Chloe's arm, and guided her hand with the bandage. 'Hold.'

Next he adjusted the saline drip to allow more fluid through and checked the General's pupils once more. It had been a while since he'd last given Harleem analgesics and topped up the epidural, glad he'd set that up before things had gone crazy. He also gave Harleem some more midazolam as the last thing he needed was his patient regaining consciousness while he was performing surgery. 'Hang in there, Harleem,' he instructed. 'I'll get you through.'

Michael opened drawers, looking for the instruments and equipment he'd brought with him. When PMA had informed him the VIP might require hernia surgery, he'd wanted to be prepared for such a situation as this. Well, not *exactly* this, he corrected himself, as no one could have foreseen the plane being sabotaged.

'Electricity would be nice,' he murmured, as he opened one locker after another, pulling out the things he'd need.

'I'll just go hook up the generator,' Chloe replied drolly.

'Funny. Hey, did you find the fuel leak? You never told me.'

'As I recall, you were being rude.'

He smiled at her words. 'I was, wasn't I?'

She waited for him to apologise but it didn't come, which made her dislike him all the more. Arrogant pig.

'So I take it the fuel leak isn't going to ignite and blow us all up?'

'Correct.'

'Good. If you can hold the torch and retractor, I should be able to do the rest. I mean, I can't do much without retraction and light. I take it you've done surgery before?'

'Yes.'

'Qualified surgeon?'

'No.'

'Let me guess, you've done several courses.'

'Working out here, you get to be an expert in a lot of things.'

'No doubt.' He handed her a pair of gloves after pulling on his own. When Chloe removed her hand from the bandage, he checked beneath and shook his head. 'I need to get this sorted now, but hopefully the bleeding is all we're going to have to deal with. If the bowel has ruptured, we'll be in for an even bigger clean-up job.'

Pulling on a mask and picking up a scalpel, he glanced at Chloe. 'I'll try and be clear in my instructions. My theatre sister often reminds me that the staff can't read my mind.'

'Thank you.'

He wasn't sure whether she was still mad at him or not, but at the moment it didn't really matter. After a brief nod he made a laparotomy incision and Chloe held the torch and the retractor when Michael had put it in place. He took the torch from her for a moment and had a good look at what was happening. Dawn was beginning to break but he needed more light. Shaking his head, he gave the torch back to Chloe and packed the wound with gauze, trying to soak up the excess blood so he could get a better look.

'Pull the retractor back a little bit more.' Michael peered more closely. 'I need light.'

'Well, this is all we've got.'

'Yes. I realise that,' he snapped, and then exhaled harshly. 'I guess this is what they mean when they talk about operating in the field.'

Chloe nodded but didn't say anything.

Michael removed the gauze and managed to see where the blood was coming from. 'Gotcha!' He reached for the locking forceps and clamped first one and then the other artery. He dabbed at the area with the gauze. 'Move the retractor just a bit. That's it. Thanks.' The excess blood soaked into the gauze, giving him a clearer view so he could suture them off. Once this was done, they both stopped and took a breath.

'Right. This isn't going to work. I need you to be assisting me, not just holding the torch and retractor.' He glanced around the plane. 'If we could suspend the torch in some way…'

'Why not see if the General's wife can hold it?'

He frowned. 'This area is very small. We can barely stand side by side.'

'That's the quickest solution I can offer.'

'Fine.' He stepped from the table with his hands held

up. 'Let's get her over here and explain the situation. Hopefully, she's not the queasy type.'

Chloe called to Kirsa and told her what they needed her to do. One look at Kirsa's wide eyes and pale face made Michael decide otherwise.

'Plan B,' he muttered, ripping off his bloodied gloves before reaching for a packet of tubing. Looping the centre of the tube around the torch, he secured it with a knot, then tied one end of the tube to the top of the General's drip stand and the other to one of the locker doors. He adjusted the end around the drip, turning it into a slip knot, then stood back to admire his handiwork, satisfied when the torch stayed suspended over the General. He looked to Chloe, expecting her to praise him for his ingenuity, but instead she merely held out another pair of gloves to him.

'What's next, Doctor?' Her gaze was cool and impersonal and Michael snatched the gloves from her.

'We finish fixing Harleem. I'll be using Lichtenstein's tension-free hernioplasty procedure. Are you familiar with it?'

'Can't say that I am, but I have resected a bowel before. Do you have any polypropylene mesh?'

'I brought everything I'd need.'

'Good. Then let's get started.'

'Fine.' He ground his teeth. The woman was insufferable. 'Have you given anaesthetics before?'

'Yes.'

'Administer something stronger than the midazolam.' With that, he turned to check his equipment. Usually he performed this operation in a sterile theatre environment with at least five other people in the room to assist him. This was going to be different but challenging, and he liked that.

He closed his eyes for a moment and started to visualise the surgery. First he needed to ensure the proximal part of the peritoneum was removed from spermatic structures so the mesh could be easily placed. Next he might need to ligate the inferior epigastric vessels to improve vision of the indirect inguinal hernia and then set about putting things to right. Untwisting the herniated section, applying the polypropylene mesh and doing a general check of the area to ensure the General wouldn't have further trouble was all that would be left to do.

'Do you often perform operations with your eyes shut?' Chloe's words washed over him and his eyes snapped open.

'Anaesthetic under control?

'Yes.'

'Good.' He shifted the suspended torch to the best position and began, being precise in his instructions to Chloe, and was surprised when quite a few times she pre-empted his needs. She may drive him crazy, both with her attitude and her alluring scent, but one thing he knew for certain—she was a good doctor.

By the time they finished the operation, the sun was definitely peeking over the horizon and the rumbling thunder was getting closer. It hadn't been easy, only having two pairs of hands, but they'd made do. Twice during the procedure Kirsa had spoken, and Chloe's calm and reassuring voice had answered her.

As soon as Michael announced he was done and was ready to close the wound, Chloe ripped off her gloves and went to check on Smith and West, leaving him to finish up. He tried hard not to think of how much she could aggravate him, especially as he hardly knew her. She hadn't mentioned the operation and how they'd coped well, working together. He shrugged, realising she was probably more used to making do rather than having the latest equipment at her fingertips.

He frowned as he reversed the anaesthetic and checked the General's vitals. Kirsa came up and stood near him, but didn't speak. What was the use? He didn't speak Tarparnese and she didn't speak English—at least, he didn't think she did.

'Harleem is going to be fine,' he said, but she merely shrugged. Michael made the 'OK' sign, with his finger and thumb in a circle, and Kirsa nodded. He couldn't remember whether Chloe had taken her vitals, but she was standing and quite aware of what was happening, which was definitely a good sign. Still, Michael went to wind the blood-pressure cuff around her arm but she shied away. 'I need to make sure you're all right,' he said, but Kirsa just shook her head.

He needed Chloe to either translate or do the obs instead. He left Kirsa holding the General's hand and headed to the cockpit. There, he found Chloe lying on the floor, squashed between the seats, attending to West's legs.

'Chloe?'

No response.

'Chloe? Are you all right?'

'I'm fine.' She sighed as though his interruption was the last thing she needed. 'What do you want?'

There was no need for rudeness. 'I need you to take a look at the wife. She won't let me near her.'

Chloe mumbled something and he thought it sounded like 'Smart woman' but he couldn't be sure. She started to wriggle out and, instead of watching her gorgeous body squirming around on the floor, he turned to Smith and pressed his fingers to the man's carotid pulse. His eyes widened when he didn't find one.

'He's dead.' At her words he turned and saw her tear-stained face as she stood up as best she could. Michael swallowed.

'I'm sorry.'

She shrugged. 'You were right. There was nothing we could do.' Pushing past him, she went to look at Kirsa. Michael turned to West.

'I'm sorry for your loss,' he said, placing his hand gently on the man's shoulder, and West nodded, his face pale and drawn.

'Guess it was Smithy's time to die.'

'We all have one,' Michael said quietly, he himself having cheated death quite a few times—or, at least, that was the way he saw it. Today had been yet another example. He glanced at Smith. All the survivors owed their lives to the flying skills of the man whose life had been taken.

'When's mine?' West asked, managing a weak smile.

Michael's reply was firm. 'Not today.'

'You sure about that, Doc?'

'No one's ever sure.' Michael looked up as he felt something wet land on his cheek. 'Looks as though the rain's here, though. We'd better get something to keep it off you.'

Michael saw West glance over at Smith. 'Yeah,' he said quietly, before closing his eyes.

'Back in a moment.' Michael stepped carefully back through the plane to the lockers. He'd seen space blankets in there earlier and that should at least offer West some sort of protection from the water dripping through the smashed windscreen.

Chloe looked up as he came in. 'Everything all right?' He saw the anxiety on her face.

'West's fine. It's raining,' he said, as though that explained everything. He gestured to Kirsa. 'How is she?' He rummaged in the lockers, getting to know the contents quite well.

'Shaken up but fine. I've just done the General's obs. Everything's good.'

'Thanks.' He withdrew a space blanket. For some reason the animosity that had sparked between them throughout the entire operation had seemed to disappear. Was their situation finally getting to Chloe? Was she all right? She had a gash on her forehead. Was that giving her some pain? Or was it Smith's death and her inability to help him that was now mellowing her?

'I'll help you rig something up to keep West dry.'

She needed to be doing something, he realised, and, quite frankly, he didn't blame her. Keeping busy was what they needed to do until they could figure out their next move.

'Sure.'

'What if I go out and we put something over the outside of the windscreen?'

'With the rain, the nose of the plane might be a bit slippery. Besides, how will one of us get up there?'

'The nose of the plane is quite low to the ground. It would probably be best if I did it as I'm lighter than you.'

'It might not be safe.'

'What about our present situation *is* safe?'

'Good point. OK. What did you have in mind?'

She reached for a blanket and handed it to him, taking the space blanket from him. 'I'll go outside with this and cover the windscreen. We can secure it with some tubing inside the cockpit.' She started to undo the light he'd rigged up over the General as she spoke. 'I guess it doesn't matter if Smith gets wet, and if we can angle the shelter to perhaps block West's view of his buddy, that wouldn't hurt either.'

Michael nodded. 'Sounds like a good plan.' He went to the open door and once more helped her down the steps, leaving her to jump the last one to the wet ground below. He went into the cockpit and waited, looking for places to secure the tubing. Within seconds Chloe had managed to carefully climb a tree right beside the front of the plane and was precariously on the aircraft's nose.

It took some effort and a bit of time to get the shelter into place, but by the time they'd finished, the space blanket was blocking as much rain as possible from entering. West was now being kept dry and, as Chloe had suggested, they'd managed to bring the silver blanket down to block West's view of Smith.

'That's it, Chloe. Good work,' Michael called. 'You all right to get back inside?'

'Right as rain,' Chloe called.

West chuckled and Michael found himself smiling. 'Didn't you think that was funny?' West asked.

'I thought it was customary to groan at bad puns, rather than laugh.' Michael returned to the door and waited for Chloe. When she appeared, her blonde fringe plastered to her face, her ponytail hanging limply at the back, she just stood there.

'Coming in?' he asked, and held out his hand.

'I'm just going to check the fuel leak again to make sure everything's all right.' The thunder rumbled overhead. 'Now that the sun's up, I can see what's really happening. I also just want to take a look around. Perhaps I can figure out where we are.'

'Why don't I come out, too?' He wouldn't mind, especially as things seemed settled with their patients.

'Stay with the patients. I won't be long,' she said, and disappeared from view. She needed a breather. To be away from him. That plane was way too small and it was starting to drive her crazy. The rain didn't bother her in the slightest, as she was used to being rained on in Tarparnii. Walking around the plane, Chloe checked the fuel leak and was pleased to see it being washed away by the now steady rain.

She continued her way around the plane and then headed up the slope of the mountain, panting as she climbed higher. When she'd been walking for about ten minutes, she turned and looked back down at where she could see the tip of the plane's tail. Her eyes widened as she realised what she was seeing.

Although Smith had done some very fancy flying to put them down safely, he'd apparently put them down in the only clearing he could find—a clearing that had been formed by a previous mud slide.

Chloe sighed in frustration. Couldn't they get a break? Frustrated tears stung at her eyes and she sniffed. With the way the rain was currently pouring down, showing little sign of stopping any time soon, the precarious ground the plane rested on would soon turn into a slip-and-slide. The plane would become unstable and slip right down the side of the mountain.

That wasn't their only problem. With the bodyguard admitting the plane had been tampered with, she wouldn't be surprised if a search party was currently under way to find them. If someone wanted General Ualdarin dead, they were going to make sure of it.

She sat down in the dirt and buried her head in her hands. This was more than she could handle. First being forced to leave the place she loved, then being faced with the pig-headed yet intriguing Michael Hill, which hadn't helped the situation at all. Those two things she'd been able to cope with, but sabotage? Plane crashes? The death of her colleague?

No. Life wasn't being very fair at the moment. The worst thing was that even though she hadn't liked what she'd seen of Michael Hill so far, she felt drawn to him. Being attracted to a man she didn't like was ridiculous. When he'd come into the cockpit and realised Smith had died, Chloe had wanted nothing more than for him to pull her into his arms and comfort her. She shook her head. It was stupid. What she felt for him was stupid. This whole situation was stupid. She didn't even know him yet how could she continue to have this…need to be near him?

She was shaken up. Out of sorts. Delusional. Stressed—yes, that was it. Her attraction to him could be attributed to the stress they were under, what they were going through. They were both doctors, which meant they needed to work together, to do whatever they could to help the others.

That was it and the sooner she figured out a way to get them out of that plane and to somewhere safe—somewhere with other people around—the better.

Lifting her head and wiping her eyes, Chloe swallowed and straightened her shoulders. She could do this. She was strong. She had survived a lot in the past and she would survive this. Just as she was about to stand, she thought she heard a noise behind her.

Freezing, she looked around, not moving her head and listening carefully for any further noises. It had sounded like a branch snapping, as though someone had stood on it. Was someone else around? Had the bodyguard's friends found them so soon? She took some calm and steadying breaths. It could just be an animal. Yes. Or one tree branch falling on another. That often happened. Be brave, she told herself, before slowly rising to her feet.

'Do not move,' came a deep Tarparniian voice, and for a second Chloe froze in fear, before opening her mouth and doing what came naturally.

CHAPTER FOUR

MICHAEL heard the ear-splitting scream and knew instinctively it was Chloe.

Why had he let her go off by herself? He'd just finished taking the General's vital signs once more and now rushed to the cockpit. 'West, I'm going after Chloe. She's in trouble.' Without waiting for an answer, Michael raced down the steps, jumping to the ground and looking about him, trying to get some sort of bearings.

In which direction had the scream come from? He wasn't sure. Blood was beginning to pump like mad around his body, and he felt the surge of adrenaline he usually equated with doing something dangerous but fun. This was not fun—but it could be dangerous. Had someone seen the plane go down? Had they come looking for them? Were they friendly?

Michael saw a muddy footprint on the ground and realised it was Chloe's. She'd headed up the mountainside. As quickly as he could, he made his way through the dense foliage, slipping a few time on the leaves and bark which were littered everywhere. He was glad he was in such good physical shape as he continued upwards, puffing hard. He could hardly call out her name, although her safety and well-being were the only thoughts on his mind at that moment. He had to get to her. He had to make sure she was safe. The sensation was both strange and possessive at the same time, although right now he didn't have the brain power to ponder it further.

Up ahead, he heard voices and he stopped still, before darting behind a tree trunk and crouching down. The voices were headed this way and he wondered if Chloe was with them—whoever they were. He strained, listening hard. Next, he heard laughter, which caught him off guard. They were getting closer now and he swallowed, trying to control his heavy breathing lest it gave him away.

In the next instant he heard feminine laughter, which didn't sound at all forced. Chloe? Was that Chloe? Was she all right? He decided not to move, not to give away his position, just in case. A second later, they came into view. There were three men, all dark-skinned and all speaking their guttural native language. Chloe was in the middle of them. One of them, an elderly man with greying hair, was holding her hand to steady her as they made their way down the mountainside—and she was smiling. That feature hadn't been a part of the picture that had entered his head the instant he'd heard her scream.

Relief was the first emotion to flood through him. Relief at discovering she was all right. Hard on its heels came anger at her having made him worry in the first place. He shook his head and stood up, revealing himself just below them.

All three men turned. Two of them were carrying spear-shaped weapons, all of them tense and ready for action.

'Michael?' Chloe's voice radiated her astonishment at finding him there. 'What are you doing? Are the patients all right?'

'They're *fine.*' He brushed a hand down his trousers, trying to ignore the way her voice washed over him, relaxing him further. He didn't want to be relaxed about her. He didn't want her smiles, the way her brown eyes brightened, the way she was making him feel. He didn't want any of it. He joined them as they walked down the mountain. 'I heard you scream.'

'And you came?'

Why did that surprise her? Did she think he was an unfeeling brute?

'I thought you might be in danger.' He glanced at the three men. 'Obviously I was wrong.'

One of the men, the one who was assisting Chloe, smiled and spoke in heavily accented English. 'Forgive us. We no mean to startle you. I am Jalak. We are friends of Chloe.'

'I'm Michael Hill, Chloe's colleague,' he said with a brief nod.

'They saw the plane go down and came to check it out,' Chloe supplied. They were almost back at the aircraft and where Michael had previously wanted to get out of the plane to stretch his legs, he now couldn't wait to get back in out of the rain. It wasn't cold—just annoying and wet.

'I've worked in Jalak's village many times.' Chloe smiled at the men around her and Michael found himself frowning. He hadn't realised she was such a flirt but there she was, charming all three men so much that they'd probably do anything for her. 'Anyway, Jalak has sent one of his party back to the village in order to get more men to help us with our patients.'

'Thank you,' Michael said, directing his comments to the elderly man. When they arrived at the plane, they all walked around the craft, Michael getting his first glimpse of exactly where they'd landed. The ground was relatively clear of trees and he realised that where the pilot had put them down was a site where trees had been crushed by a previous landslide. The area around the plane was starting to become heavily drenched in rain.

'We need to move the patients,' Chloe said from behind him. 'It's just too risky with all this rain.'

'Agreed.' He watched as the Tarparniian men started to board the plane, leaving their spears outside. He and Chloe started towards the door and she slipped, losing her footing and bumping into him. His arms instantly came around her, trying to make sure they were both steady. The moment he touched her, the moment her wet skin rubbed against his, he couldn't help the low moan that escaped his lips. Her wet body was pressed against his chest, almost relaxing against him as though she, too, enjoyed being exactly where she was.

She slowly turned her head and looked up at him, their gazes meshing. They were both giving and receiving unspoken messages and when her lips parted, her breath now coming out in small, shallow gasps, it was all Michael could do not to capture her mouth beneath his and take everything she had to give.

It was a strange sensation all right. To want this woman—a woman he didn't even like. Well that wasn't strictly true. From what he'd seen of Chloe…whatever her name was, there was a lot to admire. And a lot to discover about her.

A call from inside the plane broke the moment and Chloe quickly pushed away, totally embarrassed as she made her way to the plane. If they hadn't been interrupted, she would have let him kiss her. She had *wanted* him to kiss her, which was in itself totally ridiculous. She wasn't interested in him. Attracted maybe, but not interested. A woman could be attracted to a man, she thought as she hefted herself up the first step then continued on into the plane. A woman could look but not touch.

But you *did* just touch, she reminded herself, and shook her head in disgust. 'Jalak? What's wrong?'

'The General.' Jalak pointed to where Harleem lay, Kirsa still standing by his side holding his hand. 'That is my General, is it not?'

'Yes.'

'And he is all right?'

She was just about to cross to the patient to do the obs when Michael's deep voice washed over her from behind.

'He's doing just fine. We've had to operate on him but I'm anticipating he'll make a full recovery. Let me check his vital signs and get him ready to be transferred. Chloe, why don't you take Jalak into the cockpit and ask him how he thinks we might extract West?'

'Good idea,' she said with forced brightness, anxious to be out of Michael's presence. Even a temporary reprieve might help her wayward thoughts. He shouldn't have touched her. Why had she let him? She could have pulled away, she *should* have pulled away, rather than leaning up against him, feeling his strength, the safety of his arms, being unable and unwilling to move away.

Why had she let him touch her? They needed to get this ball rolling, and fast. She needed space, distance and preferably other people around if she was going to control this instant attraction she felt for her new colleague. And control it she would.

'All right,' she said in Tarparnese. 'We'll need to cut the co-pilot out of his seat somehow—his foot is badly crushed but we need to do what we can to save it.' The Tarparniian men nodded, eager to help.

Half an hour later, with Harleem and his wife *en route* to Jalak's village, Chloe and Michael had managed to pry most of the debris away from around West's crushed foot. Jalak and one other man had stayed behind to help, providing them with a crude saw from their village, which did the job of cutting away the metal, but it was slow going.

Michael was lying on the ground, his large, long frame twisted at an awkward angle as he tried to move the saw back and forth.

Chloe shook her head, her impatience growing. 'This is taking too long. Let me in. I'm smaller than all of you.'

'I can do it.'

'It's not a question of whether you can do it or not, it's a matter of size,' she snapped in exasperation. 'Your hands are too big to work fast enough in that small gap.'

Michael wriggled back and looked up at her. 'I hardly think that warrants your tone.'

Chloe sighed and closed her eyes. 'You're right. I apologise. I'm just—'

'Anxious,' he finished for her. 'I know.'

She stepped back into the main cabin so Michael could get out. She didn't want to touch him at all if she could help it because right now she had to concentrate on her job, rather than the tingling feeling he evoked every time he got too close to her.

She waited until he was well out of the way then worked her way down to the ground and picked up the saw. The pain medication Michael had given West was definitely doing the trick so their patient was all right to just sit there and be as still as possible.

Michael watched her and conceded her point. Being considerably smaller gave her an advantage, making her better suited to the job. She was a brave one, this Chloe whoever, and Michael could feel his admiration growing by the second...as well as his frustration. How could a woman frustrate and attract at the same time?

They were definitely working against the clock and he knew that the plane shifting at any moment, the muddy ground starting to slide again and the tree outside the cockpit window teetering on the verge of coming down were all risks they had to contend with. They had to get West out and that meant calling a truce to whatever it was that existed between them.

'Almost through,' she called to West. 'We'll have you out of here in two shakes of a lamb's tail.'

'Lambs? I don't see any lambs.' West joked weakly. 'But if you bring one in, I'll definitely shake its tail.'

'I think we gave you too much happy juice,' Chloe said as she kept working. She held her breath, putting more effort into it and finally, *finally* she was through. She breathed a sigh of relief and reported the news. 'I need a new set of bandages now, a pair of gloves and some surgical tape.' Taking a blanket in her hands to protect them, she carefully pushed the last of the debris away from West's foot and leg.

There was blood everywhere and for a moment she thought his foot had already been detached, until she made out the shape. It had been completely crushed and any hope she might have harboured about his foot being saved vanished. She cleared her throat and focused.

'How are you holding up, West?' She hoped her voice sounded bright and in control because she certainly didn't feel that way.

'Still on the happy juice, babe.'

Chloe smiled and nodded. 'Good to hear.' Michael handed her the things she'd requested and she quickly pulled on the gloves before opening the packages containing the sterile bandages. She applied them to the destroyed foot and once the bandages were on, she wrapped a blanket around the area and called to Michael. 'Ready to move him now. Is everything organised?'

'Everything's ready.'

It was a squeeze to remove their patient from the cockpit and onto the stretcher, but they managed and before he was taken out into the rain, Chloe wrapped another blanket around his entire leg to protect it.

She was in the process of doing West's vitals when a loud creaking sound made her freeze. Her eyes were wide as her brain registered what that sound meant. 'Move. Move it. We need to get out of the plane *now*. Grab the stretcher. Come on,' she urged. *'Move!'* Jalak and the other man hurried out of the plane.

Another creak came and this time the plane actually shifted. 'Come on, come on.'

'Chloe. Come on,' Michael called, heading for the door and holding his hand out to her.

She looked frantically around them, grabbed the last blanket from the cupboard and began throwing bandages and syringes and anything else she could find into it.

'What are you doing?'

'We'll need these supplies,' she said, as the plane gave another creak.

'Chloe!' Michael was at the door, holding his hand out for her, but she was like a madwoman. Did she want to kill herself? Growling in anger and frustration, he heaved several bags of saline and the instruments he'd brought with him from Sydney into the blanket. 'Now let's go.'

'Almost.'

Michael wasn't waiting for her any more. He certainly had no wish to die—which was an interesting thought in itself and one he knew he'd ponder later, but right now he needed to get his crazy colleague out of danger. Grabbing the blanket in a bundle, he picked it up and heaved it out the door.

'Michael!'

'You're next.' With a firm grasp on her arm, he all but yanked her to the doorway. The plane lurched one more time but this time kept on sliding. With his heart pounding wildly against his ribs, Michael hauled Chloe close to him, his arms a band of steel around her, and with one almighty spring leapt from the plane.

They landed on the ground with a thud, rolling over a few times in the mud before stopping, both of them sprawled with their legs and arms entwined. They'd landed at the base of two tree trunks, effectively trapping them in a secure place. They could hear the sounds of the plane as it continued its journey down the mountain-side, trees broken and crushed in its wake.

Staying still for a moment, unable to believe their very fortunate escape, Chloe slowly became conscious of his heart beating beneath her ear. His chest was firm and his body was warm, despite the mud and rain covering them.

She felt…safe. Pressed against him, his arms around her. She felt incredibly safe and that was such an odd sensation for her to be feeling. The last time she'd felt this way had been just after her marriage to Craig, and that had been six and a half years ago—before her world had come crashing down.

Chloe didn't want to be attracted to Michael. She hadn't asked for it and she certainly didn't want it. She wanted peace and tranquillity and to keep on surviving the obstacles life threw at her. She wanted to help other people, to make a difference in their lives. She hadn't been able to help her husband or her child, but in the years she'd been working with PMA she'd helped a lot of people and she loved it. She thrived on it and she wouldn't let Michael Hill ruin everything she'd worked so hard for, simply because she was attracted to him.

Still…she found she didn't want to move.

'Chloe?' His voice was deep and concerned. 'Are you hurt?'

'I…um…I don't think so.'

'Good.'

'How about you?' she asked.

'I don't think anything's broken.'

'So you think it's…uh…safe to move, then?' Why was she breathless all of a sudden? It was ridiculous and the knowledge that she couldn't help the way her body responded to him only annoyed her further.

'Just a moment,' he said, his arms tightening around her. 'We should make sure we haven't broken anything.'

Chloe swallowed. 'Hmm.'

They lay there, neither one moving, as though they'd finally been given permission to enjoy the attraction between them. Michael was astounded at how scared he'd been for Chloe's sake when he'd realised she might have been swept away with the plane had he not grabbed her. It was probable she wouldn't see it that way but he'd felt the need to take action, and action he'd taken! Holding her now, feeling her body against his, was enough to make him not want to move for a very long time. In fact, he could quite get used to the feeling of her in his arms, and that didn't sit at all well with his lifestyle.

After everything he'd been through, after all the chemotherapy and change of habits, he still found it a challenge every day to maintain control of his life. Becoming seriously involved with a woman wasn't part of that plan and he knew instinctively that Chloe was the type of woman who definitely wouldn't settle for a short-term anything.

Chloe sighed and knew she had to move or else she'd want to stay in Michael's arms for longer than was practical. 'I can't believe we jumped,' she said eventually.

'We?' He angled his head and looked down at her. 'What's this *we* business? You wouldn't have made it out if I hadn't dragged you.'

'Hey. I was getting there.' She felt the stirrings of anger begin to boil and this time she did move, but only slightly. His arms were still around her and, given their precarious position, she realised if they moved too suddenly, they might dislodge themselves and get caught in the mud.

'You took way too long. It was very foolish.'

'Foolish!' Chloe gave his chest a thump. 'It was under control. The last thing I needed was to be man-handled and thrown from the plane.'

'Manhandled?' He loosened his hold and shifted ever so slightly so he could look down at her. 'I never man-handled you, sweetheart.'

'Don't call me that.'

'I saved your life.'

'What?' Chloe's temper was gearing up to full swing and she wasn't sure she cared much about the mud slide now. What was important was to put distance between herself and this arrogant half-wit before she completely lost it. 'You did not save my life.'

'If I hadn't thrown you out of that plane, you'd be in a worse position than you are now.'

'Aha! So you admit you threw me out of the plane.' His arms had loosened but she was still pressed hard against him, his thigh warm between her own. She shifted and managed to lift her head to glare down at him. The moment she did, she realised her mistake.

Their faces were only millimetres apart and she could now feel his breath on her face as he spoke.

'That's right. Misconstrue my words any way you like. Well, that's just fine, *sweetheart*. You do what you need to do so you can sleep at night. I'm happy living with…the…real…er…truth.' As he'd been speaking, he'd become aware of just how close her mouth was to his, and he loathed himself for mumbling like a teenager.

The woman was driving him to distraction. Now she was looking at him, her eyes soft and caressing as her gaze flicked down to his mouth and back again.

Her lips parted. It was all the confirmation Michael required and within another second he'd cupped his hand behind her head and urged her mouth to meet his.

CHAPTER FIVE

THE first touch was tentative, testing and terrific. Chloe's eyelids fluttered closed and she all but sighed into the kiss, wanting to explore, to tease, to make Michael feel everything she was so she wasn't stuck out on that limb all on her own.

His mouth moved slowly, taking his time as though he was trying to memorise every contour, every tiny section of her lips. Their breath mingled as they instinctively opened their mouths wider, both desperate for more.

Heaven only knew what it was that existed between them, but feeling so right when everything was so wrong was something neither wanted to consider. All that mattered was now, this second, this moment in time, when they needed exactly the same thing.

She was highly aware of her body pressed so firmly against his, the way they seemed to fit so perfectly together. Swallowing, she touched her lips to his again, enjoying the soft exploration. She was glad he wasn't rushing her but instead allowing her the opportunity to just take her time, to not be overwhelmed by new and dormant emotions. Having his mouth against hers, the way he'd somehow been able to bring forth feelings and emotions she'd managed to repress for years, made her not only feel wanted but also highly feminine... And Chloe hadn't felt that way in an extremely long time.

Sweet. How it could be possible to find such sweetness in the midst of such turmoil and tragedy, Michael didn't know, but there she was. Sweet and delectable and very alluring. It was a wonder he'd resisted her for this long. Her mouth was glorious against his, making him wonder if he could dare to dream again. For so long he'd held himself apart, not wanting to get involved with the world but pushing himself to the limits within it. Now, with the most amazing woman in his arms, her mouth on his, he felt hope begin to rise once more.

Her head was wet, the end of her ponytail now dripping with water, her clothes wet and stuck to his, and he knew he wouldn't have it any other way. Letting out an unsteady breath, he gently moved his hand against her head, making sure she didn't go anywhere just yet and wanting to deepen the sensations buzzing through him.

Slowly, so he didn't scare or frighten her, he opened her mouth a fraction more and this time allowed his tongue to tenderly touch the edge of her lips. She shuddered, and when her tongue mimicked his actions, he couldn't help but groan. Still holding himself in check, not wanting to rush ahead, he explored further, tracing the contours of her luscious mouth, his arm tightening perceptibly about her. He didn't want her to pull away, to move, to go anywhere. For now, here was right, here was comfortable, here was...exciting and new.

Michael had done many crazy and wild things during

the last four years, searching for the ultimate adrenaline rush, but he'd never experienced anything as electrifying as this. Her mouth was sublime and he knew he could spend hours teasing and testing and never getting tired of it.

'Chloe.' Her name was on his lips and she kissed it off. Michael took her mouth, but briefly this time as sanity started to return. He hated this part, the part where logic reigned. He knew he couldn't ever get seriously involved with a woman and he had no right to even give Chloe reason to believe it would be so. He kissed her one last time and shifted, feeling for the first time the sticks and rocks pressing into his back. 'Chloe,' he said again, and this time she slowly relented and pulled back, her eyelids opening in a lazy fashion that made him want to repeat everything they'd just done...and more.

'Hmm?'

'We should move.'

'Move?'

'The ground is, well, a little uncomfortable and... er...' He stopped and cleared his throat. 'We should get moving.'

Sanity hit Chloe like a brick, her gaze widening in shock at what she'd done. She'd kissed him! She'd kissed another man! She hadn't kissed anyone since Craig. Of course, plenty of men had tried to pursue her but she hadn't been interested. Why on earth had she done this now?

Chloe shifted, becoming increasingly aware of just how firm his body was beneath hers as she tried to scramble off him. It was very difficult to do, but finally she was standing and, refusing to wait for him, she marched up the mountainside. It was the one she'd climbed earlier that day when the sun had only just risen. Now, though, it was starting to get dark, especially with the dark clouds and rain, but it didn't bother her. In fact, she welcomed the darkness. That way, she wouldn't have to look Michael in the eye.

Chloe stopped, knowing she had to wait for him. They'd already become separated from Jalak and his friend, who were carrying West's stretcher back to the village. It wouldn't do for Michael to be left alone in the jungle. Especially when there were hostiles about. Glancing over her shoulder, she could just see him, walking slowly up the mountain. Couldn't he hurry it up?

She closed her eyes and shook her head. Why had she let him kiss her? That wasn't like her at all. He wasn't right for her, wasn't even her type, and yet when his mouth had touched hers, she'd willingly given in. Chloe raised a hand to her cheek and wasn't at all surprised to find her skin was hot. Drat the man! How dared he make her feel like this! She didn't want to feel this way and now every time she looked at him she'd remember. Remember the way her body had felt against his, the way his lips had moved over hers, the way he'd sought a response and received one.

As he drew closer, she realised he was carrying something and it was then she remembered the supplies she'd been adamant about rescuing from the plane. Shame and frustration swamped her, not because she'd left it to Michael to carry everything but because she'd been so wrapped up in her own emotions she'd forgotten about her job. How could she have forgotten about her job? It had been her sole focus for the past four years. These people, this land, this country. She loved it and she loved being able to help others. It was why she'd insisted on stripping the plane as much as possible. Out here, they needed everything they could get, yet Michael had managed to make her forget everything—and her dislike of him grew. How dared he deflect her from her mission?

When he'd almost reached her, she began walking again, knowing she should probably give him a hand with the supplies but deciding instead to let him carrying the burden for a while.

'I hope you know the way to the village.'

Chloe kept walking, looking around her. She had hoped that Jalak might send someone back to get them but, with the sun going down earlier these days, that might not happen. Walking around the jungle at night, especially with the people who sabotaged the plane most likely out here, too, wasn't the safest thing to be doing.

All of this, of course, didn't help Chloe to answer Michael's question. 'It can't be too far,' she finally said.

'What?' He stopped and put his blanket bundle down. 'Then why are we walking? Shouldn't we just wait for someone to come and find us? Walking around is only going to get us more lost.'

'Or land us in the village in time for the evening meal.'

'But you don't know which way you're going.'

'They can't be too far. Remember Jalak sent word back to the village and within an hour people showed up at the plane.'

'So you're saying the village is half an hour walk away.'

'Give or take.'

'In which direction?' he said pointedly, and Chloe

looked at the ground. She'd found it difficult at first to meet his gaze but then his attitude had made her completely forget she hadn't wanted to look at him at all.

'Jalak will send someone back for us.'

'Then we should wait. Besides, this…' he pointed to the supply blanket '…is heavy.'

'Aw. And a big, strong man like you can't carry it? Poor baby.'

'Hey. This is the age of equal opportunities, sweetheart. You want to carry it, be my guest.'

Chloe merely looked at him and then the bundle before turning away once more. 'Fine, then. We'll wait.'

She ignored his self-righteous chuckle.

'All right. Well, let's see if we can't find a place a bit more sheltered than this to wait it out.' Michael looked around at the dense tree trunks. They were large, tall trees, their trunks not excessively wide but very sturdy. To his left there was a cluster of about five which should provide a bit of shelter from the incessant rain. Not willing to discuss his decision with Chloe, Michael hefted up the blanket and headed over.

'Where are you going?' she asked, but he just kept on moving. 'That's too far away from the track,' she pointed out a moment later as she followed him.

'Track? There's a track?'

'We might not see whoever Jalak sends to find us.'

'We'll see them.'

'It'll be dark soon.'

He pointed to the bundle he'd just dumped on the ground. 'You threw in a torch.'

'Did I? Oh, good. But we can't use it.'

'Why not?' He turned and placed his hands on his

hips and she could tell he was getting to the end of his tether.

'Because of the General's enemies.'

'Of course.' He threw his arms in the air. 'I give up. All right? I give up. This has to have been pretty close to the worst day of my life.'

'You think I'm enjoying myself?' she countered. 'Because I'm not.'

Michael sat down in the middle of the trees, glad to have a small amount of respite from the rain. 'Going to come join me?'

Chloe looked over to where he was sitting and then back to where they'd been standing a few minutes ago, unsure what to do next. If she sat with him, there was no telling what might happen. She'd kissed him once. She might do it again—even though she didn't want to, she told herself firmly.

If she stayed closer to the path, at least she'd be able to see whoever came to collect them and it would also provide her with distance from Michael. That was definitely the safest option. She guessed that, given the time since they'd jumped from the plane, West should be safe at the village in about ten more minutes. Give them thirty minutes to get back and they'd have their guide. True, they'd be walking back in the dark but, as Michael had pointed out, they at least had a torch.

In answer to his question, she turned and headed back to the path—well, it was sort of a path but it was the way Jalak had come and found her that morning so that was definitely their best bet.

'Suit yourself,' he called. 'But you'll keep getting wet.'

'I'm already wet,' she pointed out matter-of-factly. 'Besides, I'm more than used to it.'

'But why be wet if you don't have to be?'

There was no reply and Chloe sat down, resting her back against a tree trunk and closing her eyes. Hopefully, Michael would keep quiet and let them wait this time out in peace.

The next thing she knew, she was woken with a start and realised she'd fallen asleep. The next second, she had a hand clamped across her mouth.

'Shh.' Michael whispered close to her ear. 'It's only me.' He removed his hand.

'What are you doing?' she snarled. 'You scared me.'

'Shh. Someone's coming.'

'Well, of course they are.' When she spoke in her normal voice, Michael clamped his hand across her mouth once more. She hit his arm and somehow he managed to grab both her hands in his free one.

'It's not your friends,' he whispered firmly in her ear. 'Now, keep quiet.'

Dread coursed through Chloe, her eyes widening as she understood what he was saying. When she nodded, he removed his hand and quickly helped her to her feet.

'Come back to the trees with me. It's too exposed here.'

Again she nodded and allowed him to carefully lead her. He was crouching down and she realised he had the torch on, shining it close to the ground to show him where to step but also not to attract attention. As they came to the cluster of trees where she'd left him, Michael sat down and Chloe realised he'd cleared the area of sticks and leaves, making it smooth and ensuring they didn't make too much noise. He switched off the torch.

'I fell asleep,' she eventually said softly.

'We both did. Rough day at the office, I guess.'

'Who's out there?'

'Like I said, not your friends. Listen.'

Both of them sat there, straining to hear. Chloe was just about to say she didn't hear anything when she heard a male voice.

Michael leaned forward and whispered in her ear. 'Can you tell what they're saying?'

Chloe shook her head. 'Still too far away. I'd guess they're still halfway down the mountain but their voices are carrying up to us.'

He nodded. 'If it had been your friend Jalak, he would have come from above us.'

'Yes.'

'OK.' He paused and she almost felt him hesitate before he said, 'Stay close.' Then he put his arm about her, drawing her to him. It was a little difficult not to be close as the cluster of trees really only provided enough room for the two of them and the blanket of supplies.

'Hopefully, whoever it is will find the plane and call it a night,' whispered Chloe.

'They'd guard it, wouldn't they?' Michael asked.

'Yes. That way they can take a good look in the morning. Either that or they'll blow it up.'

'Terrific…because a bush fire is one thing missing from this fantastic day we've had.'

Chloe smiled in spite of herself. 'This isn't Australia, Michael. The rain is steady and will contain any fire that might start. No bush fires with all this moisture about.'

'Good point.'

Chloe quietly cleared her throat before asking, 'How long did I sleep for?'

'Not sure. I dozed off myself.'

'So someone from the village may have come looking for us?'

He shrugged. 'Who knows? Perhaps they learned of the search party below us and decided it was too risky. Besides, they have the General to worry about and keep safe.'

'Jalak would have sent someone if it had been safe. Oh, no. That means something's happened.'

'You don't know that for sure.'

'I know it better than you do.' She stopped, catching herself before she said something she'd regret. Now was not the time. Instead, she felt her inner bubble begin to break. The tension just snapped and everything they'd been through since meeting, the arguments, the plane crashing, the General's operation, Smith dying—everything—right up to Michael hauling her off that plane, passed quickly through her mind and she realised enough was enough and let the tears flow out.

Turning her face into Michael's chest, she began to cry quietly. His arms tightened as her body was racked with sobs. He didn't say anything—just held her, and it felt...good. Very good. Too good—but now was not the time to be dealing with her emotions. Crying would help release the tension so she could think more clearly but the emotions would have to wait for further analysis.

When she stopped and was hiccuping now and then, he placed a brief kiss on her head.

'Relax,' he said when he felt her tense. 'Let's just rest for now.'

'I'm not going to let you kiss me again,' she whispered on a sigh.

'I have no intention of doing so,' he replied, and Chloe wondered why she found that so offensive. 'Let's just sit here quietly and wait the night out. In the morning, we'll figure out our next move. Right now, I'm too exhausted for anything, even kissing.' He yawned as though to prove his point, his arms shifting to gather her closer.

'In the morning,' she echoed, pushing aside her confused feelings and closing her eyes, the lub-dub of his heart lulling her to sleep.

CHAPTER SIX

THE next time Chloe opened her eyes, it was definitely daylight. She was warm and cosy, pressed up against Michael's firm body, the blanket draped over them. She frowned, not remembering pulling the blanket over. Michael must have done it. His consideration was overwhelming and she realised there were deeper layers to the man than she'd previously thought. Sure, he came across as arrogant and even a bit domineering, but perhaps that was more of a barrier against people finding the real Michael Hill.

She, of all people, knew about barriers. She'd erected quite a few since her husband's death and for the most part she was happy to live behind them, only ever opening up to people she completely trusted. She paused at that thought, listening to the steady beating of Michael's heart. Was he someone she could trust? Could she share her innermost pain and secrets with him?

Chloe frowned, still quite astounded by the way she was almost coming to depend on him. When she was with him she felt safe, and while that was definitely a nice feeling it was also one she hadn't felt in years. To feel safe and protected. It really was something she'd been missing, although she hadn't realised it until he'd crashed into her life.

She blinked, taking in their surroundings, and realised that the sun was higher in the sky than it had been yesterday when she'd initially climbed this mountain. How long had they slept? She wasn't sure, and as she didn't wear a watch she couldn't check.

Michael, however, did wear a watch, and she twisted slightly so she could reach for his hand which was currently around her waist, holding her close. Her eyes widened and she froze as she felt where his arm should have been. Instead of nice warm, soft skin, she encountered cold reptilian scales.

Instant panic rose within her but she controlled it enough to stay as still as possible, hardly daring to breathe. She looked down and, sure enough, there was something moving, gliding slowly beneath the blanket, and now she could feel it going across her legs.

Closing her eyes, she clenched her teeth and worked double time to control the need to shudder. 'Michael.' She said his name slowly but firmly, not wanting him to move—just to wake up.

'I see it,' he said softly, and she almost passed out with relief that he was awake. 'Just keep still and it won't bother us.'

Chloe opened her eyes and could now see the head of the snake coming out from beneath the blanket and going off into the jungle. The body of the snake was still travelling across them and she swallowed, keeping her reactions in check. Of course she'd seen several snakes and other reptiles during her time working in Tarparnii but she'd never encountered one this close before.

Finally, the body thinned out and the tail went across her waist and down her body, going over her leg before appearing at the end of the blanket and then disappearing into the jungle.

Still, neither of them moved. Her entire body had broken out in a sweat and she swallowed again. This time she didn't stop the shudder that passed through her and in the next instant she heard Michael's deep laughter.

'Well, that was certainly a novel way to start the day. Different and, at the moment, better than yesterday.'

'Hmm.' Chloe rubbed her hands together and then wiped them on the blanket. 'I could do without that ever happening again.'

Michael chuckled again and moved her forward so he could stand up. When he did, he twisted and stretched his arms above his head, and Chloe was mesmerised by the actions. From where she was sitting on the ground, he looked so tall and lean, his shoulders firm and broad. His muddy, slightly torn business shirt had become untucked from his trousers and his hair was all messy. When she'd initially boarded the plane he'd been wearing a tie, but at some point he'd removed it and she couldn't remember when. Not that it mattered—except that she was starting to notice insignificant details about him and that only lead to trouble.

He ran his fingers through his hair, giving his head a good scratch, leaving his hair sticking up on end. 'At least the rain's stopped.'

So it had. That she *hadn't* realised and she shook her head in disgust. It wasn't like her to be so preoccupied but, she rationalised, a lot had happened to her in the past twenty-four hours and the fact that the same things had happened to Michael provided them with a unique bond. It was bound to heighten their emotions, to let them seek comfort and even give in to other basic needs. It was a common effect when faced with this type of trauma. Feeling more comfortable with this rationale, Chloe carefully picked up the blanket and stood, shaking it out.

'I don't remember you getting the blanket last night. Where did you put the supplies?'

Michael pointed to a bush beside them, its soft foliage pressed down beneath the weight of the stuff. 'It got a little cold around three o'clock.' He'd woken to find her shivering a little in his arms and although their bodies had provided quite a lot of heat, it hadn't been enough. So he'd carefully removed her, sorted out the blanket and then repositioned himself, happily gathering Chloe back into his arms.

He'd been glad she'd slept through and when he'd been holding her, listening to her steady breathing, he'd placed a kiss to the top of her head, amazed at how right she seemed to feel in his arms. He'd felt it before, when they'd jumped from the plane, but this was different. Simply holding her had given him such calm pleasure and quiet satisfaction and he hadn't experienced those emotions in a very long time.

Still, he knew Chloe wasn't the woman for him. Not in the short term, and there wasn't even an option for long term. The fact that he had flawed genetics was enough to keep himself under control when it came to relationships. Never would he put a child of his through what he'd been through. It was unfair, not to mention cruel, but deep down inside he couldn't do it because of the suffering. Watching his child go through the treatments he'd needed to have would be agonising.

'I don't remember.'

Chloe's words brought him back to reality and he looked at her, deciding he should lighten the atmosphere by teasing her a little. After everything they'd been through, it was important to try and find some humour. 'You were definitely out of it. Do you know you snore?'

'I do not.'

'Now, if only I'd had a tape recorder. Why didn't I pack my Dictaphone?' He smiled and it was then she saw the teasing glint in his blue eyes.

'Very funny.'

'For you perhaps. Me? I had a headache most of the night.'

'Stop it.'

He dipped his head and met her gaze. 'Do I have to?'

Chloe's breath caught in her throat at his look. He was incredibly good-looking and it was no wonder he had her hormones in a tizz. She forced a smile and waggled her finger at him as though he were a little boy. 'Yes, you do. We have work to do.'

'And what is that?'

'Figuring out what to do next.'

'That's easy.'

'It is?'

'Sure. We bundle up all the supplies and head on up the mountain. We should be able to pick out paths and hopefully your friend Jalak will send someone to meet us.'

'Let's hope so.'

Michael casually draped his arm about her shoulders. 'Trust me.'

'Now, that *would* be dangerous.'

His laughter was so spontaneous that she found herself joining in, gazing up at him. When he pressed a brief kiss to her lips then let her go, the laughter died instantly and she was glad he'd turned away to take care of the supplies so he wouldn't see the stunned look on her face. She wished he wouldn't do that!

Neither of them spoke again as they started to walk up the mountain. The heat of the day was starting to make itself known and Michael longed for a long cool shower or even a bucket of water so he could have a blanket bath. Still, he was here, he was alive. He doubted he'd ever stop marvelling at surviving the plane crash. It was strange. Where he'd constantly put his life in danger, wanting to experience the thrill, the rush— anything and everything to prove himself truly alive— he now felt life course through him as he walked through a jungle, his clothes sticking to him, trying to think of something to say to make Chloe smile again.

She had the most beautiful smile and he wished she'd do it more often. He hadn't meant to press that kiss to her lips, especially when he knew he was supposed to be distancing himself from her and the way she was constantly making him feel.

'Recognise anything?'

Chloe shook her head. 'No. Sorry.'

He shrugged, tightening his hold on the blanket. 'Don't apologise. It's not your fault you don't know this jungle like the back of your hand.'

'But I should. I've worked here long enough.'

'Chloe, I've lived in the same district my whole life and two weeks ago discovered a small pizza shop in one of the back streets that's been there for thirty years. Besides, I'll bet that during your time here you've usually had someone from PMA or one of the villages guiding or taking you to places. Am I right?'

'Yes. Actually, you are.'

'There you go, then. Also, I think PMA and the villagers prefer you to concentrate on what you do best.'

'Are you patronising me?' she asked, and Michael was taken aback.

'No. Not at all. Why would you think that?'

'Oh, probably because you're highly arrogant, think a lot of yourself and can be a little abrupt at times.' She shrugged.

'So you think just because of those bad points— which I totally refute—that I'd patronise you?'

'I don't know.' She threw her arms in the air. 'I don't know you.'

'True, but you can get to know me.'

'What? Now?'

'Sure.' He motioned to their surroundings. 'We've got the time, we've got the place. Why not?'

'So—what?—we just casually tell each other our life stories? Is that it?'

'If that's what you want.'

'Me? I didn't start this silly…game.'

'Whoa. It's not a game and getting to know one another is hardly silly. We're going to be stuck with each other for the next few days at least, or so I'm guessing. I doubt even PMA would have put together the paperwork for another flight to leave the country.'

'True.'

'How about I go first, then?' When she didn't reply he continued. 'I was an only child. My parents divorced when I was fourteen and then a year later they remarried.'

'To each other again?'

'No, to other people.'

Chloe nodded.

'My stepmother had two boys from her first marriage, Leith and Virgil. My mother married someone almost twice her age but they're happy and he's always been decent to me and…uh…four years ago my dad passed away. I used to have a cat but she died of old age and I can't bring myself to get another one. I work at Sydney General hospital three days a week and do a private clinic twice a week. Well, that's what I did before signing up for PMA.'

'That's it?'

He shrugged. 'Isn't that enough to start with?'

'What? No favourite food, favourite colour or girlfriend?' Chloe couldn't look at him as she asked the question. She was reluctantly interested in finding out about his love life and that alone irritated her more than she cared to admit right now.

'Good point. Good point. Can't leave out the essentials. Um…sushi, blue and don't have one.'

'You don't have a girlfriend?'

'Nope. Why?'

'I don't know. Just thought you'd have been married and divorced by now—like every other surgeon.'

'Hey, they're not that bad and, no, I haven't been either—that's married or divorced.'

'Not interested in matrimony?'

He glanced at her, tripping over a small tree root and stumbling. 'Wow. For someone who didn't even want to do this, you're asking a pretty heavy question.' Now was his chance. To set her straight. To let her know that even though they'd shared some amazing moments, not the least of which being her body on top of his and their mouths pressed firmly together, he wasn't looking for permanence.

'Don't want to answer it, eh? I'll take that as a no, then.'

'Hey, look. Matrimony for other people is fine. Good luck to them.' He shook his head. 'It's not for me.'

'That's making for a pretty lonely life.'

'My choice.'

'Yet you haven't even tried marriage. How do you know it's not for you?'

'Why all the questions on marriage?' He looked over at her. She was becoming almost adamant about it. 'Have you ever been married? Is that why you're hiding yourself away in the jungle?'

'First of all, I'm not hiding and, second, it's none of your business.'

'What happened? Marriage went wrong? He cheated? You cheated?' He raised his eyebrows as he said the words.

'And you think that's the only thing that could break up a marriage?'

'They're the most common. Well, apart from death, I guess, but—' He stopped and turned to look at her. Chloe kept walking, ignoring him. Michael swallowed over the sudden dryness of his throat, feeling like a right royal jerk. Her husband had died. He opened his mouth to apologise, to try and fix his gaff, but at that moment

Jalak came around the bend and Chloe broke into a run, throwing her arms around the dark-skinned elder.

'I am sorry,' he said in his deep accented English. 'It was not safe last night. I am glad you are both well. Meeree has been worried.'

'Meeree?'

'My *par'machkai*,' Jalak supplied. 'My wife.'

Michael glanced at Chloe but she refused to look at him. He'd upset her yet again, although this time it had been unintentional.

'You were wise to wait last night.' Jalak took the bundle from Michael and then started walking back the way he'd come. 'We are not too far from the village.'

He was right for five minutes later Michael saw a clearing up ahead and realised they were entering the village. As they neared, he saw several huts around the edge of the clearing, each with a small garden with native flora. The huts appeared to be made with bamboo poles, leaf-woven screens for walls and thatched triangular roofs. The huts were also raised from the ground and slatted walkways linked all the houses together. Smart, given the amount of mud they encountered. Chickens and goats were loose in one corner, children were playing in another, and all about there was life and laughter.

As soon as they were spotted, several children and young teenagers came running over, all of them embracing Chloe like a long-lost relative, with several of them holding *his* hands and arms and chattering away in their native language, bright smiles on their faces.

'There they are.' A woman who spoke excellent English came over holding both her hands out to Michael. 'I am Meeree,' she said, taking his hands in

hers. She gave his hands a little squeeze. 'This is the traditional Tarparniian greeting of welcome and you are
very welcome in our village, Michael.'

He felt very out of depth but gave her hands a little
squeeze in return. 'Thank you.' It was obvious they'd
been discussed as everyone seemed to know exactly
what was going on. Everyone except Michael.

'How are the patients?' Chloe asked, as she headed
over a large patch of green grass to a particular hut.

'They are well,' Meeree replied. 'Belhara and Bel
have been caring for both our honoured guest and the
young man.'

'Let's take a look.' Chloe walked up the wooden
steps into a hut and Michael could do nothing but
follow. It appeared she wasn't going to tell him what
was going on or what she was doing, and he realised she
was still annoyed or upset with him over his earlier
comment. Even though his remarks hadn't been
designed to cause pain, they'd not only reminded Chloe
of her past but she probably wasn't happy that he'd ac-
cidentally guessed her inner pain. Losing a loved one
wasn't at all easy—he knew that all too well, but it had
been his father who had died and, as close as they had
been, it wasn't the same as a spouse. From what he'd
learned about Chloe since they'd met, she seemed an in-
tensely private person and he wanted to somehow let her
know that he would not only keep her confidences—
should she decide to talk about it—but that he also
understood…to a certain degree.

As they entered the hut, he realised this was their
makeshift hospital. It was one large room and their two
patients were on stretchers which were propped off the

ground with bamboo frames. In one corner was a table with a large washing bowl on top and towels. Next to it were open shelves containing various medicines and equipment and a neat pile of blankets.

Jalak took the supplies they'd rescued from the plane to the shelves and started unloading. The hut was neat and orderly with light coming in from the two open windows, which had fine mosquito netting over them.

One woman, who he heard Chloe call 'Bel', was leaning over the General, a stethoscope in her ears as she listened to his chest. A moment later another man entered, carrying two buckets of steaming water. He emptied them into the wash bowl before turning to grin at them, his white teeth bright against his dark skin.

He walked up to Michael and held out both his hands. 'Belhara,' he said, and Michael greeting him warmly, introducing himself. Belhara pointed to West. 'You operate?' Chloe turned and spoke in Tarparnese and Belhara nodded and moved out of the hut.

'What did you say?' Michael asked as he crossed to her side.

She slowly raised her gaze to meet his. 'I said I would be operating. He's gone to get things ready.' With that she turned away and engaged the nurse in conversation, effectively leaving him out.

Meeree put her hand on Michael's arm. 'Come outside. I will show you our village.'

Michael frowned but did as he was asked, wondering idly just how much village there was left to see. Once they were outside, Meeree took him to the centre of the village where there was a well and told him how PMA had provided it for them. She pointed out the different gardens where they grew their produce and also a smaller hut where everything was stored.

'You must not be angry with Chloe,' she said. 'She is very dedicated and now she must think.'

'About what? The operation?'

'The pilot, his foot is not good. There is no blood.'

'Yes. He'll need an amputation.'

'Chloe Fitzpatrick is a very special woman to this village. We all love her and she loves us. Understand, she is on a difficult journey and one that I feel is soon coming to a close.'

Fitzpatrick! Yes, that was her surname. 'What journey?' he asked. 'You mean with PMA?'

'No.' Meeree smiled as though he were a naïve child. 'Her journey. We are all on a journey. It is what life is about. One journey ends as another begins. Some are long, some are short. You, too, are on a journey. You have known great suffering and you are like Chloe, keeping people away.'

His eyebrows hit his hairline. 'How do you…?' He was stunned. He'd known this woman for all of two seconds and already she'd summed him up—and had done it accurately as well.

'I am a woman who sees deeply. Be there for Chloe. She needs to have someone to care for and that someone must care for her in return.'

Michael looked over to the hut where Chloe was, and saw them taking the General out. 'What are they doing?'

'He must be moved so Chloe can operate. She would not have moved him if he was bad. He is fixed now, our leader.' Meeree turned to him. 'You did good. You have saved our leader and for that we all offer you our thanks. You are always welcome here, Michael Hill.'

'Well, I'd liked to examine him.'

'There is no need. Bel has nursed him and he must leave. It is not safe. Help Chloe.' Meeree patted his arm. 'Come. You must talk as doctors.'

They returned to the medical hut and Michael was surprised at the transformation. Sheets had been hung in a square to create a barrier. When he looked inside them, West was still lying on the stretcher, being watched by Belhara. Chloe and Bel were at the wash bowl in discussion.

Michael walked over and cleared his throat. Slowly she turned and looked at him.

'Need some help?'

'Yes. Have you done an amputation before?'

'I assisted once when I was doing my internship in orthopaedics.'

'Good. I'll lead, you and Bel will assist and Belhara will administer the anaesthetic.'

'Do you have everything you need?'

She nodded. 'The instruments are being sterilised and will be brought in soon.'

Michael was impressed once more. Chloe was definitely in charge and he liked it that she knew exactly what she wanted and needed. 'Will you be speaking in English?'

'Most of the time. Belhara doesn't understand too much English so I'll get Meeree to translate so everyone knows what's going on and then I can concentrate on the operation rather than having to repeat myself in both languages.'

Meeree stepped forward. 'I will say what you say in my language and vice versa. Shiny?'

'Shiny?' Michael frowned and Meeree smiled.

'Sometimes I may use the wrong word. Although in our language the word for perfect or happy translates better into the word shiny.'

Michael nodded. 'Shiny. I like that.'

Chloe asked Meeree to check on the instruments and when she was told they were ready, she gave Belhara the signal to begin the anaesthetic. As West already had a drip in, it was easier to administer the medicine through that line.

Chloe began scrubbing her hands and Michael watched her, knowing she was going through the entire operation in her mind. It was what surgeons did and his admiration for her grew. She seemed to be doing that a lot, impressing him. Perhaps because it was rare, in his experience, to find a woman so dedicated, so driven and professional in her approach to everything. She was also wound a little too tight and could do with letting go and having some fun once in a while. Although he recalled she hadn't been so prickly when they'd kissed. She'd definitely let herself go then and it had been an amazing experience.

'Ready?' she asked, when he'd finished scrubbing.

He nodded and as they entered the operating area both were completely focused. Chloe cleared her throat. 'I'm going to talk my way through this,' she announced to everyone. 'That way, we're all on the same page.' She said this first in English for Michael and then to Bel and Belhara in Tarparnese. 'Meeree?'

'Yes, I am here,' Meeree said from the far corner.

'I'll apologise in advance as I'll probably be slipping in and out of speaking both languages.'

'Do not worry, *Separ.* I will make sure everyone knows what is being said.'

'All right, then. Let us begin. I'll be making a trans-
verse skin incision about a hand's breadth distal to the
tibial tuberosity. It will encircle the anterior half of the
calf.' Chloe picked up the scalpel and did as she'd said,
Michael beside her, anticipating her every need. At the
medial and lateral edges, she turned perpendicularly
and continued in the longitudinal axis of the limb,
creating the posterior flap.

Not only did she need to think about removing the
bone but also giving West enough of a stump to have a
prosthesis fitted. The incisions needed to be careful and
precise, not only for the skin but for the layers of sub-
cutaneous tissue, fascia and muscles of the anterior and
lateral compartments. Michael had agreed to actually do
the sawing of the tibia and fibula, and as he did it, she remembered why she'd never really taken to orthopaedics.

Once that was done, Chloe divided the muscles of the
posterior compartment, ligating the posterior tibial and
peroneal vessels. They continued on, shaping the posterior flap by excising the soleus muscle. It wasn't long
before she was closing in layers. Two suction drains were
left in place and finally the entire operation was done.

'You were brilliant,' Michael said as they degowned,
his eyes shining with admiration.

'Really?'

'Chloe, is it really that hard for you to take a compliment?'

She shrugged. 'I guess I'm not used to getting them.'
She concentrated on pulling off her protective garments.
She then closed her eyes, put her hands above her head,
clasped her hands and then bent from the waist, stretch-
ing out her tired muscles.

Michael's gaze roved over her gorgeous form, amazed at how perfectly proportioned she was. He also couldn't believe he was standing here, ogling his new colleague. Shaking his head clear, he started to degown, averting his eyes from her tantalising body. It brought back the memory of how she'd felt pressed against him and he quickly headed from the hut, in need of fresh air.

Meeree came out a moment later and called to him.

'Michael. You and Chloe should go for a walk. Take in some fresh air. Clear your heads before the sun sets.'

'Thanks, but we need to keep a watch on West.'

'Go. He will be fine. Bel will watch over him. She is very good.' Meeree placed a hand on Michael's shoulder. 'Do it for Chloe. She needs to stop and take a breath. You have both been through much and there is more to come. Go. Relax so when you return you are…' Meeree searched for the right word.

'Shiny?' Michael interjected, smiling at Meeree.

'Prepared,' she finished, returning his smile.

Chloe walked out, satisfied with West's current condition, but stopped when she saw Meeree and Michael, smiling at each other. 'Did I miss something?'

'No,' Meeree answered. 'Now you must go, *Separ.* Take Michael to the waterhole to wash the day off you. You will feel better. Go. We will watch your patient.'

Chloe sighed, knowing West was in good hands as Bel was one of the best nurses she'd ever worked with. She also knew the waterhole was exactly what she needed. What she *didn't* need, however, was more time alone with Michael. Still, there was nothing else to do and as her gaze quickly travelled over his dishevelled form, she realised he really did need a wash. She probably looked just as bad, her clothes covered in dried mud, dirt and perspiration. The cool, fresh water beckoned and she could already imagine herself submerged in the relaxing pool. 'OK.' She nodded to Michael. 'This way.' With that she started walking off.

'Help her relax, Michael,' Meeree said softly.

He snorted with derision. 'How? At the moment, she's as prickly as a hedgehog.'

'Then apologise for being a man and she will forgive.'

He frowned, amazed. 'How do you—'

'Go. Before you lose her from your vision.'

He nodded and jogged to catch up to Chloe.

'You and Meeree seem to be getting along just fine,' Chloe said.

'She's a very…insightful woman.'

'You can say that again.'

He thought about Meeree's words and knew she was right. She may not have known exactly what had transpired between Chloe and himself but it was probably clear something definitely had due to the cold way Chloe was treating him. 'Are you two close?'

'She and Jalak are like family.'

He nodded, not surprised by her answer. 'So how often have you been stationed in this village?'

'Quite a few times. It's more central than a lot of other villages so people travel here to see us. If there's something critical, PMA will send a team to a different village but this one feels more like home to me.'

'And you were forced to leave it,' he stated. 'It must be difficult to say goodbye every time.'

'Yes.' She swallowed over the lump in her throat, wishing he wasn't being so nice and understanding. She much preferred it when they argued because then she wanted to keep her distance from him and as he seemed to have a sort of invisible pull over her, keeping her distance was becoming paramount to her survival.

'So when was the last time you were here?'

'Day before yesterday.'

'You left from here to go catch the plane?'

'Yes.'

'Had you been doing clinics here?'

'No. This was our base at that time. We'd travelled to two different villages and done a clinic in each.'

'So, this "we"? Where are they?'

'They've moved down to the southern part of the island. They'll set up at a village about this size and hold clinics, travelling out to other inaccessible places later in the week.'

'Life with PMA.'

'It's a good life,' she said defensively, and he held up his hands. He tried to hide his smile but at least, watching her just now, he had the answer to an earlier question. When she got angry, her eyes did become the colour of deep, rich chocolate, and he liked it.

'I'm not saying it isn't. It's just…different from what I'm used to.'

'Then why did you sign up?'

'Because I thought it would be good experience.'

'Look good on a résumé, you mean.'

'I'm not a résumé type of guy.'

'Then what are you?' Chloe stopped and turned to face him. 'Why were you on that plane?'

'I was asked by PMA, as my first assignment, to accompany a critical VIP back to Australia to operate on him.'

'And then?'

'And once that was done, there was to be a review and then they were planning to send me either here to Tarparnii or to Papua New Guinea, but I guess I'll find that out once I get back—whenever that is.'

'Right, but if you don't want a helps-people-in-need comment on your résumé, why do it at all?'

'Why do you do it?'

'To help people who need helping. To make a difference in the world.'

'One patient at a time, eh?'

'Something like that.'

'And running away from your past?'

Chloe raised her chin and met his gaze, not about to let him goad her. 'Just as you're running away?'

'Not running. I don't have anything to run from. I'm just…enjoying life.' He shrugged and she started walking again, leading the way through the jungle once more.

'Enjoying your life in a country in the midst of civil unrest? Interesting.' She was intrigued, though. The fact that he wanted to seek the most from his life was an admirable quality, but something had prompted it. Something big. Something like…his father's death? She knew only too well how the death of a loved one could change a person.

Neither of them spoke for a while and instead focused on the slippery, muddy ground. She was walking just in front of him so when she skidded, losing her balance, his arms were instantly around her, making sure she didn't fall over.

They stayed still for a moment. She, looking up at him. He, looking down at her. Their mouths only a hair's breadth apart. They both knew there was this frightening, natural chemistry between them, but whether or not they even liked each other was still to be tested.

'What does *Separ* mean?' His breath fanned her cheek as he spoke, and she found it difficult not to sigh. Since he'd placed that brief and friendly kiss on her lips that morning, she'd been longing for him to hold her this close again, to have their lips almost meet, to feel his firm body against her.

She didn't smile. Instead, she held his gaze, mesmerised by the desire she saw there. She swallowed and said softly, 'It's a gemstone. A precious gemstone. I confess I've never seen one but I've been told it's very beautiful.'

'Then Meeree is right to call you by that name.'

Chloe's breath caught in her throat as she quickly processed his words. 'Are you saying I'm beautiful?'

Michael raised one eyebrow. 'Fishing? You know you're beautiful, Chloe.'

No, she didn't. It had been years since anyone had called her beautiful and she realised how nice it was. The fact that Michael found her beautiful was something she'd file away and take out on cold, wet, lonely nights.

'Michael? What's happening between us?'

He slowly shook his head. 'Don't ask me questions I can't answer.'

'Can't? Or won't?' He was silent and she continued. 'It's a simple question.'

'Without a simple answer. What about you? What do you think is happening?'

'I don't know.' She closed her eyes and he saw the indecision and confusion.

Michael dragged in a breath and slowly exhaled.

When she opened her eyes again, he couldn't fight his natural instincts any more. 'The only thing I'm one hundred per cent sure of is that I want to kiss you again.'

She breathed a sigh of relief. 'Then what's stopping you?'

His eyes widened a little at her words. 'Apparently nothing.' With that he lowered his head and finally… *finally*…pressed his hungry mouth to hers once more.

CHAPTER SEVEN

CHLOE couldn't believe the sensations that coursed through her the moment Michael's lips touched hers. The power, the breathlessness, the trembling. He made her feel so feminine, so precious, and she hadn't felt that way in a very long time—if ever. Only Michael did this to her. She'd felt this way the last time he'd kissed her, which was why she had never wanted to kiss him again. *That* was a definite lie because right now she didn't want him to stop.

His mouth was soft and sensual on hers, coaxing a further response, and she was more than willing to give it. This time she was glad they were vertical because she wanted to touch him, to really feel what his body felt like to her touch. She'd been denying herself since their last kiss and now she not only had the opportunity, she had the desire.

The tingling began in her fingertips, the itch, the need to have her skin pressed against his. Carefully, she flexed her hands before bringing them towards his torso. The feel of his body through his shirt was wonderful but she'd had a small taste of that last time. If she was going to go for it, she was going for it big time, and she lowered her hands to slip them beneath the untucked fabric. The instant her fingers made contact with his smooth skin, which was covered with a light smattering of hair, she sighed with longing, a sound that was echoed by Michael as he deepened the kiss.

Her hands travelled slowly up the sides of his body before slipping around to caress the contours of his back. His physique was incredible and, as though just touching him wasn't enough, the urge to allow her lips to travel the same path as her hands was becoming more difficult to resist.

This was it. The way life should be. The way it needed to be. The way it was, and that thought petrified her. How could the sensations have increased so quickly? She'd worked hard to put these emotions, these feelings aside. She'd figured out years ago how to pigeonhole her thoughts yet Michael seemed to be slowly prising her thoughts open—without her permission.

Overwhelmed, she jerked out of his embrace, slipping a little on the muddy path again but quickly stepping onto the leaves and twigs on the other side. Her breathing was erratic. Her eyes were wild. Her lips were swollen. Michael simply stared at her in confusion and pain. Chloe turned away, unable to bear his gaze on her, and continued towards the waterhole.

'Chloe? Chloe, what's wrong?' he asked as he followed her. 'Talk to me.'

She couldn't. She couldn't keep doing this. She was creating more pain for herself because, to her utter disbelief, she was starting to care for Michael. *Really* care, and that was dangerous territory as far as she was concerned.

'Will you at least tell me how much further it is to the waterhole?'

'Not far,' she called, and he relaxed a little. At least she was going to talk to him, although he doubted whether it would be about what exactly was occurring between them.

He spotted the river up ahead. 'Is that where we're headed?'

'Yes.'

When they came to the river bank, he was surprised the water wasn't as high as he'd anticipated, especially with all the rain that had fallen yesterday. Chloe kept on walking, leading him downstream before turning right. They climbed over some rocks and she made herself concentrate on what she was doing lest she lose her footing and fall into his arms once more.

She stopped by the bank of an enclosed waterhole, which was fed by a natural spring. Michael stood beside her. 'Wow. This place is beautiful.' It had been shaped hundreds of years ago and provided privacy thanks to the rocks and trees that surrounded it. Michael swallowed as he glanced at his surroundings before finally settling on Chloe again.

A light smattering of rain started to fall and both of them looked up for a moment before returning their gaze to each other. 'Chloe. We need to talk.'

She turned her back on him. 'Not now, Michael. I just want to get into that water and get clean.'

He pondered her words, wondering if she meant them figuratively as well as literally.

'Fine.' He started unbuttoning his shirt at the same moment she glanced at him. It was a huge mistake.

She shouldn't have done it but she had, and now she found it impossible to look away, her mind going completely blank.

She watched his fingers slide the button from its hole, before moving down to the next and the next. Soon the fabric hung open and in another instant he'd dropped it to the ground, leaving his chest bare.

Chloe couldn't tear her eyes away. She wanted to touch him all over again, to feel the smooth skin beneath her fingertips, beneath her mouth as she pressed kisses all over him. She licked her lips, her gaze slowly rising to meet his. She knew he'd been watching her watching him and that only heightened the tension between them.

'Don't, Chloe. Don't look at me that way.'

'Why?'

'Because you make it impossible for me to resist you.'

'Do you want me?'

'I do.' The words were said with a deep and burning need she recognised.

'Yet it's wrong between us.'

'Yes, and we've both admitted that. You don't want this and neither do I, but it's there, Chloe. It's there and it's growing.'

Chloe swallowed at his words, her gaze travelling over his torso once more. 'I know.' She was now desperate to get herself under control. What was she doing? This wasn't what she wanted. It couldn't be. She forced herself to look away, to move away, to put a bit of distance between them.

She'd never wanted to open herself up to deep emotional hurt again. She'd loved Craig and he'd been taken from her. She'd loved Nate and he'd been taken from her, too. She couldn't do this. Opening herself up to Michael would cause too many problems, would make her feel again, and she didn't want to do that because having feelings for someone only led to pain and suffering. Besides, he'd already told her he wasn't interested in marriage and that was fine with her, yet when he held her, she could quite easily lose herself in him. It was as though he blocked out the past and the future, both of them living totally in the moment, and that was the most dangerous part of all.

'Chloe?' Michael placed a hand on her shoulder and she jumped. She hadn't heard him move. She turned and looked down at the ground and only then realised that he'd removed his shoes. His feet were splattered with dark brown mud and small pieces of leaves.

'Chloe, talk to me. We have to figure this thing out.'

Slowly, she raised her gaze to meet his. 'I'm sorry,' she whispered. 'I can't do this.'

Michael watched her professional mask slip into place once more. 'Are you scared of your feelings?'

'No.'

'That's a lie, and it's also the worst thing you can do to yourself. Believe me, I've tried to lie to myself in the past and it only ends up causing me more trouble and pain.'

'What about?'

He turned his back and walked to where he'd left his belongings, undoing his belt.

'See? You're asking me to talk to you but you won't talk to me.'

'I'm asking you to discuss what's going on between us. That's all. Getting this sorted out verbally might actually help us deal with it. If we talk about it, it will help us to understand it and then we can resist it. I freely admit that when I hold you in my arms, I forget everything. I don't profess to understand it, I didn't ask for it, but it's there. Ignoring it is only going to make it worse.'

He had a point but she didn't know how to talk about her emotions. Even with Craig, she'd kind of let him lead her through the minefield at the beginning of their relationship. When he'd been diagnosed with cancer, the talking had stopped and he'd started withdrawing from her, leaving her out in the cold, trying to figure out what was going on while nursing him as best she could.

Michael pulled his belt from his trousers before unbuttoning and sliding them from his legs. He stood there in his boxer shorts with his hands on his hips, staring at her. Chloe was hard pressed to keep her tongue in her mouth, she was so agog at the magnificent specimen before her.

'See? I can admit that you affect me, that I have strong and passionate feelings for you, but I know it can't go much further or we'll both end up in emotional places we don't want to go. So I'd like to suggest that until we can talk about what's going on between us, we keep our distance.' With that, he turned and stalked towards the waterhole. He climbed up onto one of the rocks, stretched his arms above his head and dived neatly into the water.

One second he was there and the next he was gone.

Chloe continued to stare. Was that what she wanted? Really wanted? To have Michael disappear from her life? She glanced out over the water, watching the ripples gradually subside. She liked it when he was around. She liked the way he made her feel—too much. *That* was the problem. In fact, it had happened several times since the plane had crashed. How was she supposed to concentrate when all she could think about was him?

She frowned, looking at the water again, realising he hadn't surfaced. She immediately began to shed her clothing, dropping it carelessly to the ground as she walked over the rocks until she was in her underwear. Her heart pounded wildly as she realised the rain had stirred the usually clear waters to a murky brown and that Michael might have become tangled with some of the aquatic plants near the bottom of the waterhole. She'd taken a deep breath and was about to dive in when he surfaced, over at the far end.

Chloe closed her eyes and sagged with relief. He was all right. She shook her head, proving to herself that he distracted her far too much. She concentrated on getting her breathing back to normal before opening her eyes and diving in. The cool, refreshing water felt heavenly against her body and after she surfaced, she closed her eyes once more and floated on her back, enjoying the weightlessness and the light pattering of rain on her face.

Was he right? Would talking about their feelings help them gain some perspective and understanding about what existed between them? For two people who professed not to be interested in each other, they were having a difficult time keeping their hands and lips to themselves. She breathed deeply, recalling clearly just how much she had been willing to lose herself in him. The man was even more addictive than he'd been yesterday.

Deciding she needed a break from such deep thoughts, she rolled over onto her stomach and dived beneath the water. When she surfaced, she looked around the waterhole and once more felt her heart pound in her throat when she failed to locate Michael. Then she saw his dark head on the other side and breathed another sigh of relief. He was all right. The man would definitely be the undoing of her.

She watched as he began to swim, his strong strokes knifing through the water, thanks to those firm arms of his. Memories of her fingers touching those arms, his torso, his back assailed her, and Chloe swallowed over the lump of desire that rose in her throat.

Why did the man have to be so…addictive?

It was then she realised he was about to pass her and she joined him, swimming back to their starting place. She waited while he pulled himself from the water, the desire washing down her body and exploding within her as her gaze followed his progress. His physique was second to none and she could tell he worked out regularly. The water sluiced off him and she unconsciously licked her lips.

When she eventually lifted her eyes to his, she realised he was watching her carefully, his blue gaze filled with heat. 'Chloe?' Even her name was a caress from his lips, one which she wanted to hear every day for the rest of her life.

She knew what he was asking. Just the way he said her name told her that he was willing to listen, willing to discuss whatever it was that was burning between them. How she wished she could take him up on it. She breathed out slowly and closed her eyes, breaking the contact.

When she next opened her eyes, he'd moved, although this time she didn't panic. He was pulling on his trousers, obviously her cue to get out of the water and do the same. She levered herself out and, refusing to even glance his way, picked up the clothing she'd hastily discarded and started pulling it on. She wondered if he was watching her, just as she'd been watching him, but then the thought of his gaze on her body made her start to hyperventilate so she quickly focused on the task at hand.

It was difficult to dress in wet clothes when your body was also wet and although she managed to tug her trousers on, she had trouble with her top. It had bunched into a roll at the top of her shoulders and she reached over and under to try and tug it into place.

'Here.' Michael's deep voice startled her. She hadn't heard him approach. He was a quiet one, she'd give him that.

'Let me help.' He turned her round and began to unroll her top, his fingers brushing her back on several occasions. Unfortunately for Chloe, each time they did, she couldn't help the gasp that was drawn from her. Michael eventually smoothed the top down, resting his hands on her hips. She could feel the heat emanating from him and closed her eyes, trying desperately to be strong.

He didn't remove his hands. Instead his thumbs began to move in slow, intimate, electrifying circles in the small of her back. Chloe closed her eyes and moaned with pleasure, astounded at how easily this man affected her. She wasn't sure whether he was giving her another chance or whether he was just unable to resist being this near and not touch her.

When he slowly drew closer, his chest pressed against her back, she leaned against him, grateful for his support. Michael's strong hands still held her firmly, his fingers sliding around to her stomach. Leaning over her shoulder, he gazed down to where the edge of her top was stuck, just below her bra. With his breath fanning her neck, causing goose-bumps to ripple over her body, he trailed his fingers upwards and gently tugged her top down into place.

Chloe parted her lips, her breathing so erratic it was difficult to control. How could he set her on fire while completing such a simple task? When he turned his lips to press tantalising butterfly kisses against her neck, she tipped her head back, resting it on his shoulder and granting him access to whatever part of her he wanted.

'Chloe,' he murmured between kisses. He shifted her head to the other side and paid just as much attention to that side of her neck. Chloe felt her legs weaken as she continued to float on the wave of desire Michael evoked. Just when she thought she was going to explode, when she was ready to turn and promise him whatever he wanted, he put her from him.

She staggered for a moment before her legs finally supported her weight. She turned and looked at him, seeing the naked passion in his expressive eyes. 'Got to stop,' he said, and raked an unsteady hand through his hair. With that, he turned and stalked back to his shoes and belt. Picking them up, he headed back in the direction they'd come, not waiting for her.

Chloe stared after him in stunned disbelief. Had she really been ready to give herself over to the attraction that existed between them? Perhaps Michael was right. Perhaps they needed to talk it out and keep their distance. To make a plan and stick to it. He didn't want a relationship and neither did she. Surely it was as simple as that. Wasn't it?

She quickly gathered up her shoes and headed after him, surprised that when she came to the river's edge she hadn't yet caught up with him. She stopped, listening carefully for sounds, but couldn't hear anything out of place. She headed on a bit further to where the path left the river and spotted him, sitting on a wet log, putting on his socks and shoes.

With all the calm and finesse she could muster, she walked over and sat down beside him, following suit by pulling on her own socks and shoes. When she was ready, he stood and indicated for her to precede him. As they walked, neither of them spoke and he reflected on the difference between their walk to the waterhole and their walk from it. They both needed to focus their thoughts and ignore the bond forming between them.

When they arrived back in the village, Jalak crossed to them, smiling brightly. 'I talk to PMA. They will send a new plane in two more days.'

Chloe sighed then nodded. She didn't want to leave Tarparnii but knew it would be inevitable. 'Thank you, Jalak.'

'At least then we'll be able to move West and the General to a more stable environment,' Michael said.

Jalak shook his head. 'The General has gone.'

'What?' they both said in unison.

'He and his *par'machkai* have left. They know it is not safe for them here. He is safe now.'

'But I needed to check him, to make sure he was all right,' Michael protested. 'He's had major surgery. He needs more time to recover, and his wife should have been checked, too.'

'You fixed him, no?'

'I fixed him but a lot could go wrong. He could get an infection or—'

Jalak placed his hand on Michael's shoulder and said quietly, 'It is done.'

'Is West still here? Or has he been taken somewhere else?' Michael couldn't help the sarcasm. It was frustrating and annoying that when he was trying to help, trying to save someone's life, they ignored everything he said, doing their own thing.

Jalak was frowning now, not understanding properly. 'He is here.' He pointed to the hut where Chloe had operated.

'Good.' Michael broke away and went to check on the co-pilot. Chloe turned to Jalak and spoke in Tarparnese.

'He's not used to how things are done out here,' she said. 'But I do understand his frustration.'

'If the General becomes sick, he knows you are here, but our leader will survive.'

Chloe hugged the man before her. 'I know.'

Meeree came over and placed her hand on Chloe's back. '*Separ.* You had a refreshing bathe?'

'Yes.'

'I have new clothes for you and Michael. Come.' Meeree led the way to a hut close to where West was. It was a hut Chloe had often stayed in and, like the others, it was one large room where several of the PMA staff usually slept. It contained a table with a wash bowl, cooking and eating utensils, towels, blankets and sheets.

This one also had chairs and a table, making the sleeping area smaller. Two sleeping mats had been placed on the floor, side by side, and folded neatly on the mats were dry clothes.

'Thank you,' Chloe said to her friend.

Meeree held her hand for a moment and gave it a squeeze. 'You like him, yes?'

'Who?'

'*Separ,* you do not play games with me.'

Chloe sighed. 'I'm confused.'

'But you like him.' It was a statement.

'Yes, but I don't want to.'

'Why not?'

'Well, because he's pig-headed and arrogant and mildly selfish.'

'Is he? Or is that a protection?'

Chloe's mind raced over some of the conversations they'd had before nodding.

'He needs you to help him, Chloe, and you must let him do the same for you.'

'I don't need help.'

Meeree smiled indulgently. 'Everyone needs help to finish their journey.'

'I'm finishing?'

'Only if you choose.'

Chloe closed her eyes and hung her head, feeling totally drained. 'I just can't think any more.'

'Change. Eat and then sleep. I will get Michael.'

When Meeree left, Chloe struggled out of her wet trousers and top, trying not to recall the way Michael had helped her, his hands caressing her skin, making her shiver with longing. No. She couldn't think about that now. She had to be quick. He'd be here soon and she needed to be changed. As she pulled on the beautiful skirt, which she knew had been made and dyed by the village woman, she realised that she'd also started changing on the inside.

Michael was awakening desires she'd thought long gone and buried—buried with Craig. Also, she knew she was confused regarding her feelings for him, but she was also surprised to find she didn't feel guilty where she'd always thought she would. After Craig's death, she'd locked that part of her heart away, promising herself never to give her love to another man. She'd felt it would be a betrayal of her marriage vows, but now she knew that wasn't true. Death had parted her from Craig and she was no longer a married woman, which meant she wasn't doing anything wrong by admitting she had feelings for Michael.

Even as the words passed through her mind she tried to deny them, but this time couldn't. She had feelings for Michael and they were growing more intense every moment they were together. He'd wanted to understand what was between them so he could resist it, but right now Chloe wasn't sure they *should* resist, and that alone scared her silly.

She heard his footsteps outside the hut and quickly finished buttoning the cotton shirt before pulling her wet hair from the band. She fluffed her hands through the wet strands, wondering why he wasn't coming in.

'Michael?'

'You're in there?' he said, still not materialising. 'I wasn't sure.'

'Are you coming in?'

'Is it safe? I mean, Meeree told me you were changing.'

Chloe couldn't help the smile that touched her lips. That was sweet of him and something she hadn't expected. 'I'm changed,' she replied, and a moment later he came into view.

He stopped, allowing his gaze to adjust from the bright afternoon sunshine outside. He made out her form and swallowed over his suddenly dry throat at the vision of loveliness she made. When he'd asked if it was safe, she should have said no.

All he could do was stand there, all thoughts of getting out of his own wet clothes gone as he drank in her beauty. The skirt she was wearing came to her knees, showing off the gorgeous legs he'd coveted at the waterhole, but it was her hair, loose for the first time, that mesmerised him.

It was still damp but seeing it free from its band changed her facial features, softening her natural beauty which radiated out from within. He had no idea what the attraction between them meant, he hardly knew anything about her, but what he did know was that he couldn't get enough of her.

'I'm done so…I'll let you…' she pointed to the clothes Meeree had put out for him '…uh…get changed.' She wished he wouldn't look at her like that, but at the same time she didn't want him to stop. Forcing herself to look away, she bent and picked up her wet clothes and shoes, slipped her feet into some hand-made moccasins and walked in a wide circle around him.

As she passed, Michael breathed in her unique scent and closed his eyes, clenching his hands into fists to stop himself from grabbing her and hauling her against his body, his mouth longing once more for her lips to be pressed to his.

She stopped at the door. 'The clothes should fit. The guys from PMA sometimes leave clothes behind. Meeree is getting quite a collection.' Chloe's gaze quickly raked his body. 'You're about the same size as a few of them.' She turned away before she lost her focus once more.

'Thanks.' He waited until the sound of her footsteps had disappeared completely. Then he counted to twenty before opening his eyes and relaxing his body. Why did she have to be so alluring? Didn't she have any idea of the effect she had on him? He stripped off and dried himself, then pulled on the jeans and cotton shirt that had been put out for him. There were even dry shoes! At the moment, that was definitely a little slice of heaven.

When he was done, he collected his wet things and headed out, only to run straight into Chloe.

'Michael?' Chloe stopped and stared at him. The denims were perfect and hugged those amazing thighs. The shirt was a little tight across his shoulders and arms, but as far as she was concerned it was just right, showing off his amazing physique. For a moment she found it difficult to swallow.

In the ten minutes they'd been apart, her hair had dried a bit more, curling a little just below her shoulders. Unable to resist the glorious gold strands, he reached out and touched her hair, marvelling at its softness as it sifted through his fingers.

'You're stunning.' His voice was deep and filled with desire.

Her tongue came out to wet her dry lips, the longing

coursing through her begging for him to kiss her again. Instead, Michael dropped his hand and took a step away, realising she was becoming more addictive with each passing second.

She knew it was the right thing to do, to separate, to put some distance between them, and she was glad he'd been the strong one. 'Ready?' she asked, the word coming out breathlessly.

'For?'

'Food.'

He relaxed a little and nodded. 'Most definitely.'

'Good. Put your wet things by the door. Someone will take care of them.' She headed down the steps onto the grass, the light rain cooling to her warm body— warm from the repressed desire still running through her veins. 'This way.'

Even as they walked, they kept their distance. If they could just keep control for the next two days, then they'd be back in Australia, back to their own lives, where this veil that had been thrown over them would lift. It had to or she'd go insane with wanting him.

'Did you check on West?'

'Yes. I'm happy with the result.'

'I thought you would be. You did an excellent job.'

She could hear the genuine praise in his tone and she appreciated it. 'Thank you.'

'You should do surgery. You're good at it.'

She shrugged. 'I have other things I'm good at.' As soon as the words left her lips, she realised how he might misconstrue them. 'Uh…work things. Medical things,' she clarified quickly.

'I understood what you meant.'

Chloe sighed. 'Is everything we say now going to have a double meaning?'

'Possibly,' he said, his smile crooked and reluctant. 'Let's not worry about it.'

'Right.' She indicated a larger hut. 'Food has been prepared for us in here.' When they entered, they found Meeree and Jalak waiting for them. Jalak indicated a rough plank of wood no bigger than a coffee-table, which had been set for them. It contained a glorious array of foods. Fresh fruits, cold meats, bread and other delicacies he'd never seen before awaited him.

'*Jupoypu'na'wl'vaD,*' Jalak said, and bowed. 'A feast fit for royalty.'

'We're hardly that,' Chloe protested as she picked up a piece of fruit that looked similar to an apple except it had an orange tinge to the skin. 'But I doubt we'd complain.'

Michael glanced at the food and found it difficult to decide what to try first. 'Thank you.' Meeree and Jalak acknowledged his thanks then headed for the door.

'You need some peace,' she said, and they left.

Michael turned to Chloe, who shrugged and then bit into the fruit. 'Mmm.'

'This is amazing,' Michael said, sitting down in the low chair.

'They are a generous people.'

'Indeed. What did Jalak say? When he spoke in Tarparnese?' Michael asked, as he sampled something else. Never had food tasted so magnificent in his life. The tastes were the same but different and, given that the last meal he remembered having had been back in Sydney before he'd boarded the plane, it was like manna from heaven.

Chloe swallowed her mouthful. 'It's a saying reserved for either very close family relatives or people they are closest to. It means "for my beloved true friends".'

'It's a nice saying.'

'I think so.'

'I can see why you like it here.'

She smiled and took a sip from her cup. 'It's very natural. There's no pretence here. If there are disputes between villagers, a meeting is called and things are sorted out.'

'Jalak and Meeree are in charge?'

'Jalak is the headman.'

'The rest of the world seems so far away.'

'Yes.'

'I can also see why you don't like being forced to leave here. Returning to Australia and civilisation will be strange after the last few days.'

She nodded. 'And loud.'

'Yes.' Michael swallowed his drink then looked at her. 'It doesn't seem like running away when you're so happy.'

Chloe stopped in mid chew and met his gaze.

'You wanted to know if I was running away from something and I said I wasn't running,' he continued.

She finished her mouthful. 'Are you?'

'I'm trying to get control,' he said slowly.

'Control over your life?'

'Yes.'

'People who are looking for that have usually had their world shattered in one way or another.'

'That's right. Other people have no idea the lack of control we really have.'

'Is this about your father's death?'

'Sort of.'

'Was he sick?'

'Yes. Cancer.' Michael picked up another strawberry. 'We are all so blasé nowadays, probably because everyone in the world seems to be affected one way or another by it.'

'I agree. We either know someone who's had it—a family member, a friend, even a friend of a friend.'

'Or had it ourselves.' He looked away, unable to hold her gaze.

Chloe felt her skin heat and said softly, 'You've had it?'

Michael nodded. 'And I'm guessing your husband died of it.'

'Yes.'

'Well, there's something we have in common. Victims of cancer. Welcome to the twenty-first century.'

CHAPTER EIGHT

THEY both slept soundly that night but when Michael woke up in the morning, it was to a complaining back and a very sore left arm. He shifted a little, deciding he simply wasn't used to sleeping on wooden floors on top of a mat that was nothing more than woven grass. Chloe had put a few blankets down for him to lie on to make it a little softer, but he was certain he had a bruise on his hip.

When he tried to move his left arm, he found he couldn't, and opened his eyes to see what the problem was. His gaze widened as the cause of his dead arm was identified. Chloe appeared to be using his arm as a pillow *and,* he realised, his body as a hot-water bottle.

She was lying on her side with her back to him, her body extremely close to his but not quite touching. Her breathing was soft and even and her floral scent invaded his senses, making the urge to reach out and touch her more difficult to deny.

Michael wanted to stay there, so close yet so far, but the pain in his arm caused by lack of blood circulation was getting worse. He needed to move and to do that meant he'd be waking Chloe. It was the last thing he wanted to do.

After the cancer revelations, they'd changed the subject and spoken on light topics, both checking on West before returning here to their hut. As they'd had no night-time clothes to change into, they'd simply slept in what they had been wearing. Michael had been highly conscious of Chloe lying there, not far away from him, but eventually the fatigue of the last few days had overpowered him and he'd slept. Slept next to the most amazing, caring and beautiful woman he'd ever known.

It was dangerous ground he was treading on, and he wasn't sure whether it was stable or not. For years now he'd told himself he would never have a serious relationship with a woman because of Hodgkin's lymphoma. Cancer had changed his life and now he knew it had changed Chloe's, too.

It gave them something to talk about, feelings to share, because once a life had been intimately touched by the disease, emotions were stirred, views were changed and perceptions were altered. When his father had been diagnosed, it had been bad enough, but when the doctors had insisted on testing him, only to find he, too, had had the disease, though in the very early stages, Michael's world had been knocked off its axis.

He wondered what had happened to Chloe's husband. What type of cancer had it been? Obviously, he'd been quite advanced but even so, she must have been young and impressionable when she'd married. To love and lose at such a young age left long, lasting scars. She'd told him last night that she was thirty-two and he knew she'd been working for PMA for the past four years.

There had also been one point when he'd felt she'd wanted to tell him something else, something other than her husband dying, but she'd changed her mind and clammed up once more. She wasn't an easy woman to get to know but, then, he himself wasn't too forthcoming about his past so he could hardly blame her. What he did feel, however, was respect. She was not only a brilliant doctor but an incredible person, who could have easily shrivelled up and let life pass her by but instead she'd chosen to join PMA and help.

He wished his own motives for joining had been as honourable. Looking for an adrenaline thrill, as well as practising medicine in a different way, had been all he'd had in mind when he'd signed up for the three-month stint with the medical aid organisation. Now, though, having survived the last few days, he once more found his perspective shifting. Or perhaps it was seeing Tarparnii and its people through Chloe's eyes. She honestly loved it here and was loved in return. This wasn't just a job to her, and he respected that more than she could know.

He bit back a moan, knowing he couldn't lie next to her any longer, the pain in his arm becoming totally unbearable. Perhaps if he moved quickly, jerked his arm out the way one would rip off a sticking plaster, she might not wake up. Then again, she would also risk hitting her head on the hard floor.

Michael frowned and instead lifted her head with his free hand, trying not to concentrate on the soft and silky blonde tresses or the soft smooth skin of her cheek and neck. Why was the woman so irresistible?

She murmured something and shifted, turning so she was now facing him, this time snuggling right up against his body. He used the opportunity to remove his arm and gave it a quick rub, feeling the blood begin to pump through it once more. Pins and needles followed but he was past caring as his total awareness of Chloe grew.

'Mmm.' She sighed. 'Michael.'

His name was a soft and breathy caress on her lips and his own mouth curved into a smug male smile to think that she was dreaming about him. The desire to touch her was too much to ignore and, lifting his right arm, he carefully placed it at her waist, his hand sliding up her back to cradle her more closely to his frame.

Her eyes snapped open and she swallowed, her breathing increasing instantly. Michael looked at her, expecting to see relaxed drowsiness on her face. Instead, he saw total alarm and panic.

'Snake,' she whispered, when her wild eyes met his.

Michael chuckled. 'No. No snake this morning.'

'Yes. I just felt it slide up my back.'

He cleared his throat, now feeling a little self-conscious as he said, 'Actually, that was my arm.'

'Your arm?' She was still puzzled and only half-awake. 'There's no snake?'

'No.'

'It's your arm?'

'Yes.'

'Oh.'

'Does that bother you?'

'Uh…well…I guess not. I mean, so long as there's no snake. That's a good thing, right?' She wasn't quite sure what to do now. Yesterday morning she'd woken in his arms, but that had been a matter of necessity. Now she was once more waking up to find herself extremely close to Michael.

She felt silly that she'd thought there was another snake, but also felt a mixture of concern and pleasure that it had been his arm. Concerned because she liked being this close to him and pleased because he wanted to be close to her.

They both lay there, trying to be relaxed and also trying to figure out what to say or do next. He was just so close and he was all firm, hard muscle and gorgeous, and she was starting to lose count of the number of times she'd been held so near to him. Surely that was a problem, or was the real problem that she was coming to like it way too much?

'Uh-h…'

'Er…'

They spoke in unison then stopped and tried again, the same thing happening. They both laughed and some of the tension eased a little. 'I guess we should get up and go check on West,' she said.

'Yes. Although…this is nice.'

She looked up at him with a shy smile on her lips. 'Yes.'

'I like holding you, Chloe.'

'And that's a problem,' she finished for him, wondering why she felt so sad at the prospect of moving. Perhaps it was because she didn't know when she was next going to be this close to him. Perhaps it was because he'd declared no interest in relationships or perhaps it was because she herself was changing and starting to let go of her past.

Before either of them could move, a loud noise came from outside and both of them jumped sitting up so quickly they almost knocked heads.

'What was that?' Michael asked as both of them

listened. A moment later childish laughter followed and Chloe relaxed back onto the mat.

'What's going on, Chloe?'

'Word travels fast in the jungle.'

'Meaning?'

'We have visitors.'

He stilled, recalling the jungle had hostiles in it. 'Good guys?'

She smiled at that, and he felt as though the sun was shining just for him as he looked down at her. 'Yes. People have heard there are doctors here.'

'They've come for a clinic? Is this the way it usually happens?'

'Sometimes. Most of the time it's more organised, especially if we're immunising.'

'What is that noise?'

'Kids.'

'Kids make that noise?'

'They do when they all bang sticks against a tree trunk. It's a game they play.'

'And why are there kids doing that at this hour of the morning?'

'To welcome the kids from the surrounding villages.'

'Ah.' He stood and walked to the window, peering out into the daylight. Sure enough, there seemed to be people everywhere. The local villagers were coming out to welcome the visitors. 'Duty calls?'

Chloe joined him at the window, running her fingers through her hair, trying to finger-comb it. 'Something like that.'

Michael glanced at her at the same moment she closed her eyes and tipped her head back, tugging on a few knots with her fingers. 'Don't do that, Chloe,' he groaned, and her eyes snapped open at the repressed desire in his tone.

'Do what?' She grimaced as her finger caught another knot.

'You're irresistible,' he said, and planted his mouth hungrily over hers.

Chloe's eyes widened in momentary surprise but then she melted against him, placing her arms around his neck, knowing this was what she wanted, to be near him once more, to be pressed against him, to be feeling like a young, desirable woman again.

He broke off. 'I'm sorry, Chloe. I know I shouldn't but—'

She placed a finger across his lips. 'Shh. I understand.'

'You do? Then explain it to me.' He shifted away and raked his hand through his hair. 'We haven't yet discussed what's going on with us. We need to do that.'

'So we'll understand?' she said. 'I don't think that will make a difference, Michael.'

'It will. It has to.'

'So you can get control again?'

'Yes.' He hooked his thumbs into the pockets of the jeans, and with his tousled hair, crumpled shirt and bare feet he looked totally delectable.

'You can't control every aspect of your life.'

'I can try.'

'Why?'

'How can you ask that? I told you last night I'd had cancer. It takes away all your control, it runs your life, dictates what treatment you need, how you spend your time and your money. It takes away your choices in life, takes away the thrill of feeling alive.'

'And that's what you've been trying to get back. The control, the choice, the need to feel alive.' A lot of his previous behaviour now made total sense. The arrogance, the bossiness, the need to understand.

'Don't you feel it, too? Cancer changed your life. Maybe not directly and I'd never wish that on you—or anyone for that matter—but how can you not strive for control?'

'I guess I do to a point, but it doesn't consume me.'

'Then what does?'

She thought for a moment before deciding to take a chance and trust him. 'The need to survive.' Her voice was soft but clear.

He nodded. 'What about living? *Really* living. Is surviving enough?'

'For now. I guess.' He had a point, she conceded. Ever since she'd met him, she'd realised she was doing just that—surviving—and she'd become good at it. Being held in his arms, having his body close to hers, his mouth making her feel so cherished and feminine, Chloe had started to realise there was so much of life she was missing out on. In the past she'd been more than happy to miss out on those things, but now…now she was different, changing somehow, and it brought fear as well as excitement.

'*Separ?*' Meeree's voice came from outside their hut. 'Michael?'

'Yes.' They both answered and Chloe invited Meeree in, pasting on a smile, although she knew she wouldn't fool the other woman one bit.

'You are both coming to eat? We have guests.'

'So we heard,' Chloe said with a smile as she slipped her feet into the moccasins.

'Ah, yes. The children. They love to play and make noise. It is good. They must grow up far too quickly these days.'

Michael also pulled on his shoes, still thinking about the previous conversation. He really did need to understand these feelings he had towards Chloe. He also needed to get them under control. Twice this morning he'd given in to his desire to touch her, to be near her, and they'd only been awake for about fifteen minutes.

He was glad when they returned to the hut where they'd eaten last night, to find it almost filled to the brim with people and noise. Pushing all thoughts of his desirable colleague to the back of his mind, he picked up a plate and walked to the table laden with food.

Once they'd eaten, both he and Chloe went to check on West, determined to play professional doctors in order to ignore whatever it was bubbling between them.

'How was his night?' Chloe asked Bel, who had stayed with West, being relieved by Belhara at intervals.

'A bit up and a bit down, but nothing to be concerned with.'

Chloe translated for Michael and he nodded.

'Good. The drains are all still working properly,' he said, after he'd checked them as well as the IV line. They did West's observations and when both he and Chloe were satisfied with the treatment and West's response, they headed outside.

'Where is this clinic supposed to be held?' he asked.

She pointed to where Jalak and the men were just finishing putting up several tents. 'When there are this many people, it's easier to do it this way.'

'But how do you know who goes first? Who has priority?'

'Meeree will sort all that out. She will send in patients and you will treat them.'

'Just like that?'

'Just like that, and the sooner we can get started the better. You'll have one tent, I'll have the other, and Belhara can deal with anything that needs cleaning or bandaging.'

Meeree came over quickly. 'Your hands will be very full. I will start getting them into some order,' she said, before heading off.

'How am I going to know what the people are saying?' Michael asked, as they headed over to the tents. Wash basins and medical equipment was being set up. There were workers and patients everywhere and Michael wondered just how long this impromptu clinic was going to last.

'Oh. I hadn't thought of that. I keep forgetting you don't speak the language. Well, we'll just have to get Meeree to translate, or Jalak.'

'So when do we begin?' he asked, as he walked around the tent that had been set up for him.

'Right now,' Meeree said, as she brought the first patient through.

'Uh…right.' Michael quickly went and washed his hands before returning to his first patient, who was a young man of about twenty who had a large piece of wood sticking out of his leg.

'Interesting,' he murmured, and Chloe laughed.

'Good luck,' she said, before disappearing into her own tent.

Michael couldn't believe how many people came through the clinic. They were of mixed age and gender. Once, when Meeree forced him to stop for a quick break, he glanced outside and saw there were only about ten people left.

He was having a long, cool drink and a piece of fruit when Chloe joined him.

'How do you do it?'

'The clinics?'

He nodded.

'I take a deep breath and keep on going. They are pretty full on, I guess.'

'You guess?'

'Usually, though, there are about four of us, sometimes five for this amount of people.'

'Not that I'm not enjoying the challenge and the variety of cases, but this is worse than standing all day in an operating theatre.'

'Really? I'd beg to differ.'

He smiled at her. 'I guess that's why I'm the surgeon and you're the A and E specialist. It's just I'm so exhausted! I haven't felt that way since I was an intern.'

Chloe nodded in agreement and finished her fruit. 'Well, Dr Hill, it's back to work for us.' She smiled brightly at him and chuckled when he tried to move but couldn't due to exhaustion. 'The sooner we start again, the sooner we're finished.'

'You're enjoying my discomfort, my lack of experience, aren't you?' he said, as he drew strength from her laughter and followed her back to their respective tents.

'Absolutely,' she said with a cheeky grin. Chloe couldn't believe how completely free she felt. Usually, by this time the constant stream of people was wearing her down, but teasing and laughing at Michael had revived her completely. She felt as though she could take on the world.

How did he affect her in this way? He'd made her tremble and yearn. He'd made her annoyed and furious, and now he'd made her feel unique and smart. She liked the way he'd called her an A and E specialist because she certainly didn't think of herself in that role. He also had an amazing knack of making her feel precious, and she liked that, too.

They continued with the clinic and when they were almost finished, Michael heard the sound of a screaming woman. He looked out through the doorway of the tent to see an elderly woman wailing, holding something small in her arms.

Meeree was beside the woman in an instant, talking urgently and guiding her towards Chloe's tent. Michael followed, realising the woman was carrying a baby. Chloe looked up from her work as Meeree spoke in the language Michael had no hope of understanding, but from the way all the blood drained from Chloe's face, he knew it wasn't good.

Michael continued into Chloe's tent, everything happening as though in slow motion. The woman gave the baby to Chloe, who simply stood there, staring down at the child who couldn't be more than a few months old.

His gaze widened as he realised the baby wasn't breathing. He glared at Chloe, wondering why on earth she wasn't doing anything, why she was just standing there.

'Meeree, when did the baby stop breathing?' he growled, as he snatched the child from Chloe and placed it on the table in front of him, checking the airway and putting his lips over the infant's mouth and nose, giving two quick rescue breaths. Things started to speed up as Meeree asked the woman the question.

'Not long,' she answered. Michael continued with his expired-air resuscitation.

'What happened?' Again, there was a lot of talking, Meeree trying to calm the woman down enough to find out what was going on. 'Chloe?' Michael glanced at her. 'Get me a stethoscope.'

Chloe seemed to snap out of whatever trance she was in and did as she was told. Michael continued.

'I saw this baby a few days ago and the mother refused to let us treat him.'

'Here?'

'No. At another village,' Chloe supplied, listening to what was being said to Meeree.

'The mother refused treatment? Did you make it clear just how sick her baby was?'

'Yes, I did,' she said, hurt by his accusatory tone. 'If people don't want our help, we can't force it on them.'

'Want to make a bet?' he growled, but didn't say anything more. Chloe gritted her teeth, annoyed with him but far more annoyed with herself.

'She says,' Meeree said clearly, 'that she was not happy with the way the child of her daughter was breathing. She said it was thick and…' Meeree stalled, searching for the right word.

'Raspy,' Chloe provided, watching for signs of life from the child, willing it to move, to start to breathe again.

Michael didn't stop, continuing to work on the baby. She could feel the urgency surrounding him, the same drive that insisted he was not about to let this child die.

'Yes. She was on the edge of the village when the baby stopped the breathing. She was at the edge of the grass area.'

'That would make it less than one minute.'

'She said she screamed.'

Michael nodded. He had the information and now he wished they'd keep silent. 'Is there a defibrillator in case the heart stops?'

'No.'

'What?' Michael couldn't believe it. How could PMA survive without having at least a portable one?

'The team have it,' she said, answering his unspoken question. 'The team that is out doing clinics,' she clarified.

'Check,' he said, after finishing his two-fingered chest compressions.

Chloe held her own breath as she listened, hoping that there was movement, that the life was back into this tiny, innocent infant. 'Wait.'

The next instant the baby coughed and breathed in again, before letting out a weak cry, but it was enough. The grandmother collapsed on her knees and began to sob tears of relief. Meeree smiled at Chloe while tending to the woman beside her. When Chloe turned to look at Michael, she expected to see joy in his eyes. Instead, she found them cold and unyielding.

She swallowed, looking away quickly, the accusation he'd silently issued enough to bring all the guilt, all the pain and anguish back in one brief second. She'd frozen when that baby had been placed in her arms, and he knew it. Worse, she knew he knew. Shame swamped her and she could feel the food she'd not long ago eaten churning in her stomach.

'Excuse me,' she said in a whisper, and without looking at anyone she walked away.

Half an hour later, with the clinic finished, Michael walked up to Meeree.

'Where is she?' He was annoyed. 'I've looked everywhere, Meeree. Chloe's not with West, she's not in our hut or the food hut. Where is she?'

'She will be under a tree behind our hut. It is her best spot in the village. The tree leaves, they hang down to the ground, giving shelter and privacy.' Michael went to leave but Meeree detained him with a firm hand on his arm. 'Listen first.'

Michael met the wise woman's gaze and nodded once before walking off to find Chloe. It had started raining again but nothing was going to deter him from his purpose. He let his eyes adjust to the darkness of the night before carefully picking his way through the slippery, leaf-covered mud that surrounded the village. Finally, he found the tree Meeree had referred to and stopped.

'Chloe?' He paused when no reply came, shoving his hands in his damp pockets, trying to hold onto his temper. Meeree had told him to listen, well, he was willing to do that. Everyone deserved the chance to defend themselves and although he knew there was a reason *why* she'd frozen, it was still no excuse. She was a doctor, a medical professional there to help people. If she froze up every time a similar situation occurred, there could be real trouble.

It was odd. In the short time he'd known her, he'd been so impressed by her guts, her intuition and her determination. He'd come to understand her, especially after figuring out why she'd come to PMA in the first place.

'Chloe?' he tried again, his tone softening a little.

Without a word, she parted the thick foliage and reached for his hand, tugging him inside. The ground was more firm here, not as wet as everywhere else. She leaned in towards him. His hands came out of his pockets to hold her close. It was the most natural thing in the world for both of them, and he delighted in the knowledge that she wasn't going to pull away from him, wasn't going to shut him out.

Chloe stood there, content just to listen to the strong beat of his heart. He was here. He was holding her, offering comfort, despite the angry questions she knew he had. Couldn't she just take that? Just for a few minutes? Couldn't she just forget about everything else except the two of them, here, at this moment?

She swallowed over the dryness in her throat, knowing she needed to say the words out loud, knowing she needed to tell him. So many things had happened and she needed him to know the truth, to let him into the deepest secrets of her soul. She still wasn't one hundred per cent sure that she was doing the right thing but right now she needed to talk, to clear the air, to have Michael know her story.

And she needed to do it because she'd realised her feelings for Michael were much more than she'd ever thought they'd be. She not only desired his good opinion but needed it, just as she needed air to breathe. Somewhere along the journey he'd become a part of her, and while she was petrified, she also knew what she must do.

Her heart was pounding against her chest, not out of fear but out of love. She'd been afraid before to confess her feelings for him, been too scared to open up. Ever since joining PMA, she'd kept herself aloof from romantic entanglements, thinking they'd only get in the way. In some ways she'd been proved correct on that score as she hadn't been able to get Michael out of her thoughts since they'd met. In other ways it had strengthened her, helped her to grow, not only as a doctor but as a person. *Michael* had helped her to grow and she was now desperate to tell him everything.

'Michael?'

'Hmm?'

'I'm done hiding.'

He was silent and for a split second she thought she heard his heart stop. Then he swallowed and gently eased back so he could look into her face.

'I froze.'

'I know.' She didn't seem able to say anything else so he asked the question to prompt her. 'Why?'

Chloe sucked in a shaky breath before saying quietly, 'Because all I could see when I looked down at that little baby…' She faltered and looked away, telling herself to be strong, that she *had* to tell him. For her own peace of mind, she had to tell him. 'That little lifeless baby was my own beautiful boy.'

Michael held his breath, not wanting to say anything which would stop her.

'The last lifeless baby I'd held in my arms…was my son.'

CHAPTER NINE

'I JUST… I couldn't move.' One solitary tear slid down her cheek and Michael tenderly brushed it away with his thumb. Chloe wasn't there with him. Mentally, she was back at the darkest time of her life and she spoke, seeing and feeling all the same emotions as though they'd just happened.

'His name was Nate and he was my saving grace. When Craig died six months before Nate was born, I didn't think I could go on but I had to. I had a life inside me, a reminder of my marriage, of my love for Craig.' She paused for a moment before continuing. Now that she'd started, the words seemed easier to say.

'The birth was long and lonely but at the end it was all worth it. I was able to hold my little man in my hands.' Chloe looked out, not seeing anything. 'He was six weeks old and I went in to check on him. He was lying there. Peacefully.' A shudder rippled through her and Michael caressed her back, not wanting to break her concentration but also letting her know he was still there, that he was listening to everything she said.

'I think I knew. Isn't it strange? He looked peaceful

but at the same time too peaceful. I touched him, picked him up…but nothing.' The tears were flowing now, running down her cheeks, and his gut twisted at the utter desolation on her face. 'Then I had no one and it was all my fault.'

'It wasn't your fault. Your husband dying, your son…they weren't your fault, Chloe.'

'How do you know that? You don't know the circumstances. You weren't there.'

'True, but I know guilt isn't worth it. You can't change what happened.'

'I might have. I froze, Michael. Just like I did today.' She wrenched herself from his arms and took a step away, turning her back on him. 'I was a trained doctor yet when I looked down at Nate, I just froze.'

'For how long?'

'Long enough.'

'I don't believe that. How long do you feel you froze today?'

'An eternity,' she whispered.

'It was like all of ten seconds, Chloe. Ten seconds. That's all. And given the circumstances, it was also understandable.'

'If you hadn't been there today, Michael…if you hadn't come and taken over…' She stopped, unable to finish her sentence.

'You would have snapped out of it. Meeree would have snapped you out if you hadn't been able to do it yourself. Your professional side would have kicked in and taken over—which it did. The baby lived, Chloe.'

'No thanks to me.'

Michael had had it. He turned her to face him,

gripped her shoulders and gave her a shake. 'Stop it. It wasn't your fault and letting guilt—unfounded guilt—eat away at you is ridiculous. You are an excellent doctor, Chloe, and PMA, not to mention the people of Tarparnii, are fortunate to have you looking after then.' His hands gentled as he looked down into her eyes.

'You *are* a good doctor and, believe me, I'm not one to bestow praise lightly. From the earliest moments of our acquaintance, you've impressed me, and that's very difficult to do. I've become highly cynical about life since having had cancer, yet you managed to break through it to show me there are people in the world who still do genuinely care for others. You've been through an enormous amount of pain and anguish and you're still standing. You're still strong. You're a survivor.'

Chloe looked into his blue eyes and bit her lower lip. 'A survivor—yes. I've wrapped myself up in a little cocoon and forged ahead, determined to help those I can. But...'

'But?' he prompted.

'I've come to realise that surviving isn't enough any more.' She sucked in a sigh and let it out shakily. 'When Craig was diagnosed with a brain tumour, it was devastating. It sucked all the life out of him.'

'How long had you been married?'

'Two months.' She shook her head. 'He'd been having headaches but put it down to the stress of his job. The reality that he didn't have long to live consumed him, which is entirely understandable.'

'He shut you out.' Michael nodded, the emotions she talked of very real to him.

'Yes. When we found out about the baby, I hoped it would help. That it would give him a reason to keep fighting. But he was too far gone for me to reach.' She hiccuped and tears once more filled her eyes. 'He refused treatment. It was his decision, I know that, but he could have continued, he could have had longer, but he just gave up.' She sucked in another breath. 'He gave up on me and our baby.'

'Chloe.' Michael folded her to him and she buried her face in his chest and sobbed once more. 'Sweetheart.' His arms tightened, amazed at how much she'd been through and at such a young age. No wonder she'd wanted to run away, to hide herself here in the jungle where she could help people, and in return the people had provided her with the opportunity to heal her fractured life.

These tears, although heavy, didn't last as long as they had in the past, but in the past she hadn't spoken these words, these intimate fears and failings out loud. She couldn't believe she'd opened up to Michael, a man she'd known for only a short few days but with whom she felt she'd lived a lifetime. As he stroked her back, murmuring soothing words, she felt the past slip away. It wasn't out of her reach, it would always be a part of her—but that part was finished. The chapter had been written and it now had an ending.

Lifting her head, she sniffed and allowed him to wipe the tears from her cheeks. Looking at him, she took a step into her future, realising just how much she'd fallen in love with him. It was ridiculous and as the thought touched her she instantly tried to reject it—but found she couldn't. She'd fallen in love with Michael Hill…a man who had exploded into her life and turned it around.

'What? What is it?' he asked, but she shook her head, unable to confess what was so new and fragile.

'Thank you,' she finally said, and smiled up at him.

'I could say the same.'

'Why?'

'You opened up to me. That's…powerful, Chloe, and I want you to know I understand. I really do.'

'Because you've had cancer?'

'Yes, and because I've also lost someone to the disease.'

'What kind did you have?'

'Hodgkin's lymphoma.'

Her eyebrows rose. 'You're in remission?'

'That's what they tell me.'

'And your father?'

Michael swallowed, beginning to feel uncomfortable. 'He died of it.'

'Hodgkin's?'

'Yes.'

'That's rare, isn't it? I didn't think Hodgkin's was hereditary.'

Michael looked down at Chloe, hardly seeing her at all. 'I hadn't thought that either.' It was his turn to shift, to move away, to try and get some distance between this enigmatic woman and the feelings she was evoking. He didn't want to talk about it. He was more than happy to be there for her, to listen to her and help her where he could, but he did not feel the same need to be so open. He had his life under control—well, almost, but he was working on it.

He had one more day in Tarparnii before he'd be back in Australia, back in his apartment, in his life, in his control area. He would contact PMA and tell them to make sure they didn't send him back to Tarparnii—especially if Chloe was working there. She was too dangerous to the life he needed to live. She made him feel, she made him want to turn and gather her into his arms and promise her the moon and the stars and anything else that came along. She was made for happily-ever-after and as yet she hadn't found it. Instead, she'd been dealt a raw deal, but looking at her now, seeing the healing on her face, he knew she was coming to the end of her journey, as Meeree and Jalak had said. He had no problem with being the person to help her on that journey, but there was no way he was going to climb on board and head off into the sunset with her…even though a very big part of him wanted to.

Whenever he'd held her, he'd been astounded at his feelings. He wanted to protect her, to make sure no one hurt her ever again, to make sure she smiled and laughed, that she was given the opportunity to really enjoy her life, whether it was here in Tarparnii or back in Australia.

They had one more day together here and then the flight back to Sydney. Although once they were there, would he be able to walk away from her? The pull, the bond between them was becoming stronger with each passing moment they spent together, and he could feel the control he strove to maintain so fiercely slipping away once more.

He couldn't let that happen. If he didn't have control, if he wasn't in charge of everything that was happening in his life—wayward emotions included—then he knew he might crumble into a heap as his father had done— as Chloe's husband had done. He hadn't liked watching his father go through that and he'd promised himself he would always be strong, always remain in control.

'Michael?'

He turned quickly, having forgotten for a second that she was there. 'Yes?'

Chloe looked at his face and knew the mask was firmly in place. Even though she'd opened up to him, proved to both of them just how much she trusted him, it didn't mean he had to do the same thing, although she was becoming desperate for him to do so. She nodded, knowing it was better to retreat than to push him over the edge. She wanted him to talk, to reveal his past so she could understand him better but, she realised quickly, she understood all she needed to. She was in love with him and with love came a certain amount of respect for his privacy. She could guess at a lot of what he'd gone through, especially as his father had died from the same disease he'd contracted.

She held out her hand and smiled. 'Let's go.'

He was taken aback by her attitude. He'd half expected her to keep probing, to wring the past out of him until he was all shrivelled up inside, but instead she was leaving him alone. His respect for her grew and he wondered why, being a woman, she was satisfied with so little. The woman he'd been dating when he'd initially been diagnosed had begged and pleaded for him to share his emotions, to open up and express himself. It had only resulted in him pushing her away as fast as he possibly could. At that time in his life he hadn't needed therapy and while he knew deep down inside he still had a lot of unresolved issues, he would resolve them when he was good and ready and not before.

The fact that Chloe was willing to give him the space he needed, to simply open up and trust him with her own pain, without wanting deep and meaningful confessions in return, was something to be cherished. He'd known she was an amazing woman but in that moment his feelings for her intensified, which was the last thing he wanted. She was special to him—very special. It was as though she knew that if she'd pushed, he would have pushed back…back and away from her. Instead, she was willing to wait and he realised in a moment of clarity that he would tell her everything…one day.

Nodding, he placed his hand firmly in hers, before tugging her closer and pressing his mouth to hers. It was a kiss of thanks, of understanding and of respect. It was so much more than he'd ever expected to receive from a woman, and he cherished it. He cherished Chloe and couldn't believe the hope that welled up within him. He wasn't at all sure what to do with it, not having allowed himself to hope for anything except living to the next day of his life for the last four years but now…somehow she'd given him hope. Dared he even think he could find true happiness—happiness he knew he would only achieve with Chloe by his side?

He brushed the thoughts away, knowing there was a lot more to think through and now was not the time. Initially, he'd needed to understand the attraction he felt for Chloe but what he'd now come to realise was that the attraction was secondary to everything else going on between them.

When they emerged from their tree-sheltered haven back to reality, Michael reached for her hand in the darkness. 'I've admitted the baby,' he told her.

'Kapala.'

'Pardon?'

'That's the baby's name.'

'Oh. OK. I thought it was better for the grandmother and child to stay so they can be monitored throughout the night.'

Chloe nodded. 'Good thinking.'

'Let's go check.' Still hand in hand, they walked through the village to the hut where West and the baby were staying. As they entered, they found Bel cradling the baby lovingly while the grandmother slept soundly on a mat. Chloe spoke to Bel, who looked up, smiling, and nodded.

'He is good,' she said in English. 'I keep give medicine, he better.'

Michael smiled and gave Chloe's hand a little squeeze. 'Thank you,' he said to Bel, as he crossed to West's side. 'And how about you?' he said to their conscious patient. 'How are you feeling today?'

'Eager to be gone. Not that I don't love having Bel hovering around me night and day,' West said with a smile at the Tarparniian nurse. 'I'm just looking forward to a bit more civilisation while I recover.'

'Television, you mean.' Michael grinned at the man.

'Exactly. How soon can PMA get us out?'

'Day after tomorrow.'

'Good.'

'My sentiments exactly,' Michael said, and Chloe felt as though she'd just been punched in the stomach. She'd been listening to the baby's chest, pleased with the increased air flow into the lungs due to the prescribed medicine. So Michael was eager to leave the country? To get back to civilisation? She'd thought he liked it out here. Oh, not the plane crash and everything that had gone with it, but since they'd arrived in the village he'd seemed to have settled down and even appreciated what was around them—the untouched beauty of the land she loved. Obviously, she'd been wrong.

Murmuring a few words to Bel and returning the stethoscope, Chloe quickly left the hut, needing some space. How could she be in love with a man who didn't like the things she liked, appreciate the things she appreciated? He was eager to return to Australia and she knew why. Here he had no control over his life. Everything was new, everything was different, and he didn't like being forced to take yet another step outside his comfort zone. His precious control was threatened, and although she understood his need to be that way, she wanted to knock his head against the nearest tree-trunk and tell him he'd never have it.

Chloe entered the hut they were staying in and started getting the mats and blankets ready, eager to be lying down, sleeping, or at least feigning sleep, by the time Michael arrived. She didn't want to talk to him. Not now. She was cross with herself for caring, for loving him. Why, if she had to fall in love with someone again, was it the one man in the world who totally exasperated and infuriated her?

Life wasn't fair. She'd learnt that lesson very early on and it appeared she would continue to learn it. Meeree had always said she was on a journey and that the journey would soon end. She rolled a blanket up to use as a pillow then lay down and pummelled it into shape. Well, tonight her journey had ended. She'd opened up and talked about Craig and Nate and there was a distinct feeling of healing flowing over her. She'd ended her journey tonight but instead of stepping off the boat onto dry land, she'd boarded another vessel and this one seemed to be sailing right through shark-infested waters, where even more confusing emotions came out and swamped her.

When Michael finally entered, it was to find Chloe asleep, her breathing smooth and even. He longed to hold her in his arms once more, knowing he would draw comfort to help him through the night. What she'd told him about her past had also raised a lot of issues regarding his own, and holding her close would help him ignore things for a bit longer. It didn't matter that whenever she was close to him he felt more alive than he ever had before. When her mouth was on his, when her body was pressed against him, when her arms were around his neck, her fingers teasing through his hair, he couldn't think of anything else, and he didn't want to. The feelings he had for her consumed him and although he knew he should be walking—no, running—away as fast as he could for fear she would break the fine control he currently had over his life, he knew it was impossible.

When he was with her, his heart would beat as it never had before. His body would feel overcome with need and longing, and the adrenaline she could incite just by looking at him with her smouldering, desirous brown eyes was more than he'd experienced during any of the thrill-seeking stunts he'd pulled in the past.

Chloe Fitzpatrick made him feel alive. One hundred and ten per cent, all the time, and as he knelt down beside her, tenderly running his fingers through her glorious mane of flaxen hair, he knew that to be parted from her either here in Tarparnii or when they returned to Australia was going to bring a pain so intense he didn't know if he'd recover.

His eyes widened for a moment before he closed them and shook his head. 'No.' He jerked his hand away, recognising the correct word to describe his symptoms. It was love. 'No,' he said again, instantly rejecting it but knowing it to be true. He stood and walked to look out the window through the fine gauze of the mosquito screen into the darkness of night.

Falling in love with Chloe was wrong. Where he'd felt hope earlier, he now felt total desolation. Loving Chloe meant heartache for him and indeed for her, should she return his feelings. He wouldn't marry and he wouldn't have children, yet the thought of any other man being with the woman behind him made his gut twist in total agony.

The thought of leaving her, of losing her, was worse than any pain he'd ever experienced in the past. No needle, no uncomfortable scans or tests, no broken bones, no concussion, no stomach-churning, hair-losing therapy was as bad as the thought of going through the rest of his life without Chloe by his side—yet that was exactly what he knew he needed to do.

Feeling as though the walls were closing in on him, he headed for the door and sucked in the fresh air once he was outside. The village was settling down for the night, many of the visitors who had come for the clinic having stayed to catch up with friends. Others had made the journey back to their own villages. Michael sat down on the step and looked out into the darkness, feeling as though he'd lived a lifetime in the last few days.

'Michael?'

He looked up, surprised to find Meeree in front of him. 'Oh. Sorry.'

'You were away somewhere in your thoughts,' she said, pointing to the step beside him. 'I may sit?'

'Of course.' He shifted over.

'I want to thank you.'

'It was my pleasure. I'm a doctor and while I'm here I enjoy using my skills to help others.'

'I do not speak of the clinic, though it is much appreciated. I speak of Chloe. I thank you for listening to her.'

'I see.'

Meeree smiled that indulgent smile once more. 'You do not.' She turned and studied him in the dim light coming from the flaming torches around the place. 'Although maybe you do.' She breathed in deeply then let it out slowly. 'Yes. You do. You love my Chloe.'

Michael groaned and shook his head, closing his eyes once more. He wasn't used to this woman and her intuition. He wasn't used to being read so easily, often having given himself credit for hiding his feelings from people.

'You have helped her. You have listened. Now it becomes your turn.'

'Meeree, I don't—'

Suddenly, something changed in the woman and she stood, peering out into the darkness. 'Jalak.' She whispered.

'Meeree? What is it?'

'It is my *par'machkai*. My husband. He is hurt.'

'How do you know that? Are you psychic?'

'No. I care not for that. I am just an old woman with many years of experience. Jalak—I feel him. He has been my *par'machkai* for these forty years. I feel him.'

She was still gazing out blindly into the night. Michael could well understand her words. He could *feel,* as Meeree called it, Chloe and he'd only known her for the last few days.

The next instant there was the shout from afar and Meeree rushed across the grassed area into the darkness. Michael wasn't sure whether to follow or to find someone else to help him. Not wasting any time, he went into their hut and shook Chloe awake.

'Chloe?'

Her eyes opened and she sat up immediately, staring at him with wild eyes. 'What? What is it? What's wrong? Are you hurt? Are you all right?'

Michael's heart turned over at her concern but he swallowed it, pulling on his professionalism. 'Something is wrong with Jalak. Meeree says he's hurt.' He helped her to her feet and she quickly pulled on her shoes before they rushed outside.

'Where?'

Michael pointed. 'Meeree went off in that direction. If he's badly hurt, I wasn't sure where to put him. If we need to operate, where do we go? What's the protocol?'

Chloe nodded. 'We find somewhere.' There was a noise ahead of them and then into the light stepped two men, carrying Jalak. Meeree was by her husband's side, holding his hand.

'He be shot.' It was Belhara, one of the medics, who was carrying Jalak.

As they neared, Michael could see the silent tears that had streaked Meereë's face and his heart went out to her. Never before had he become so involved with his patients. They were names he saw for a certain period of time, fixing them up before shipping them back to their general practitioners for the rest of their care. Now he had a vested interest and feelings for these people and he made a silent vow to Meeree that he would take excellent care of her husband, doing everything he could to ensure the man recovered.

She met his gaze and nodded, as though accepting his unspoken words.

'Bring him through here,' Chloe said, and re-entered their hut. She put a fresh blanket down over where she'd been sleeping and knelt down to see to her patient. She glanced at Michael, knowing it didn't matter what was going on between them, he would support her and work with her to help her fix her friend—her dear, dear friend.

One of the men had used their shirt as a bandage, pressing it to the wound on Jalak's shoulder. Michael took it away, carefully touching the wound, discovering the bullet hadn't exited. 'There's not too much blood. I can get that out.'

'I have had worse,' Jalak said laughingly, but the laugh turned into a cough.

'Shh,' Chloe said softly. 'Let Michael work.'

'Chloe, can you give him something for the pain, please?'

'I am fine,' Jalak insisted.

'Shh,' Chloe and Michael said in unison, and looked at each other in surprise, before smiling.

'Belhara,' Chloe said in Tarparnese. 'Go to Bel, tell her what has happened and that we need equipment. Get some medicine to make Jalak sleepy.'

'No,' Jalak protested again, and this time his wife shushed him.

'You are not the one in charge now, my husband. Let them care for you.'

'What happened?' Chloe was the one to ask the question, although Michael had certainly been thinking it.

'Many women had come for the clinic and had no men to take them safely back,' Meeree said.

'Are they safe?' Chloe's mind raced ahead to the worst possible scenario but quickly had her fears subdued.

'They are all safe,' Jalak said proudly. 'We almost were back. It was a shock but we are now in no danger. They have gone.'

Chloe breathed a sigh of relief and was pleased when Belhara returned with the things they required. She drew up an injection of local anaesthetic, administering it around Jalak's affected arm. Just looking at it, both she and Michael could tell it would require surgery to remove the bullet but she also knew of old that Jalak would insist on being awake for it.

'We'll just let that take effect,' Michael said when Chloe had finished. 'When you're all numb, we'll get started.'

Jalak nodded and smiled as Michael crossed to a bowl of water one of the women had brought in and washed his hands. 'Chloe, can you clean the wound as much as possible? Now, let's see if everything I need is here.' He looked to the instruments before clarifying, 'Or I'll figure out how best to adapt what I have to be what I need.'

Chloe chuckled and the sound warmed him. 'Welcome to improvisation medicine.' She looked at her two friends, her gaze focusing on Meeree. 'How are you?' she asked.

'Me?' Meeree waved away her concern. 'There is no need to worry about me, Chloe. Jalak has been injured in this way many times and he will get better, just as he always does. I am not worried for him and you should not be either. I have belief in you and Michael. You are good together.'

Chloe glanced at the older woman, not missing the double meaning. Then she quickly glanced at Michael, only to find him looking at her, obviously having heard Meeree's words. Did he agree? Did he want to turn tail and run? No, wait. She already knew the answer to that question. He couldn't wait to get back to civilisation and away from her.

Scowling, she returned her attention to Jalak. She didn't need thoughts of what was happening between herself and Michael to intrude on what she was doing now. She had to concentrate on the professional aspect of her job and assist Michael simply because he was the surgeon.

She finished tidying up the wound before crossing to the wash bowl and cleaning her hands. 'Will you need me to assist?'

'Yes.' He was drying his hands on a towel and pulling on a pair of gloves. 'From what I can see, the bullet appears to have penetrated further than I'd anticipated. What do you think?'

'I agree.'

'Good. I'll administer some midazolam, which should knock Jalak out long enough for us to extract the bullet.'

'He won't like that.'

'Tough.' With that he returned to their patient's side. There was also a lot of light in the room and he realised someone had brought in hurricane lamps, which provided a luminous glow over the area, providing him with good light in which to operate.

After a few protests from Jalak and a few stern words

from Meeree, Michael watched as the midazolam quickly took effect. He studied the wound more closely, deciding on his course of action. Belhara came and knelt down at Jalak's head.

'I help.'

'Yes.' Michael nodded.

'I'll translate,' Meeree said. Michael looked at her, about to say that he didn't think it was a good idea that she stay but he saw the defiant lift of her chin. It was an action that reminded him of Chloe and it made him smile.

'OK,' he agreed. Once more, he knew that if it was Chloe who required surgery, he'd be right beside the surgeon, making sure everything was done correctly. Not that Meeree didn't trust him, but that he understood her need to be close by.

When Chloe came and knelt opposite him, things started to feel a little crowded. Still, the bullet needed to be removed despite the operating circumstances. Improvisation medicine, Chloe had called it, and he realised he liked it. It was thinking and adapting and, although frustrating at times, when it was over, the rewards were greater.

Michael cleared his throat and spoke softly but clearly. 'First, we need to turn him over. I'll then make an incision and hopefully we'll find the bullet some-where in that vicinity.' He indicated Jalak's shoulder blade. 'The scapula is probably fractured but hopefully not shattered.' He paused and frowned, his mind running through different scenarios.

'Something wrong?' Chloe asked.

'No. I'm just wishing I'd paid more attention during my orthopaedic rotation when I was an intern.'

Chloe chuckled. 'I often find myself thinking that.'

'I'm also wishing this place had an X-ray machine. All right, let's get Jalak patched up. Scalpel.' They worked silently, Michael eventually locating the bullet. Amazingly, it appeared the bullet had entered at an angle and had fractured the scapula, before travelling downwards, and was nestled in the soft tissue between Jalak's skin and the top of his rib cage.

Michael concentrated on closing Jalak's wound and bandaging the shoulder before Chloe did the vitals. 'Midazolam should start wearing off soon,' Michael commented as he pulled off his gloves. 'Make sure he has something for the pain, Chloe.' With that, he walked out of the hut.

Chloe looked at Meeree, who shrugged. 'Do I go after him?' she asked.

'Leave him for a while. He has much to think on.'

Chloe wasn't sure what had happened. One minute he was concentrating and operating and then, when it was done, he'd hightailed it out as though the hut were on fire. Had she done something wrong?

When Jalak came around, Chloe helped Meeree to get him back to their hut and settle him in for the night. 'I will care for him,' Meeree said.

'All right but you call me if—'

'I will, but he will be fine now.' She pointed to the hut where West and the baby were. 'Go to him now. Talk, *Separ.*'

'I can talk but I doubt he will,' Chloe said, her earlier impatience where Michael was concerned returning.

'You have begun a new journey, Chloe. Do not be impatient for him to find you. You still have much to decide.'

'There's nothing to decide, Meeree. The man is impossible and stubborn. He can't wait to leave here.'

'And yet you love him.'

Chloe sighed. 'I do.' She shook her head.

Meeree placed a hand on Chloe's shoulder. 'The answers will come, *Separ*. They are not far. Go,' she urged.

Michael was just coming out of the hut as Chloe approached. 'How are they?' she asked.

'Fine. Did you want to see them?'

'If you're satisfied, that's enough.' She shrugged. 'I can do the middle-of-the-night check if you like.'

'That's OK. I doubt I'll be sleeping,' he mumbled, as he headed back to their hut. When Chloe followed him he stopped on the steps outside and once more sat down.

'You're not going in?'

'Not yet. I need to wind down a bit more.'

'I understand. I have to do that after I've operated, too.' She paused. 'Like some company?'

He shrugged and she took that as a yes. Both were silent, not knowing where to start. Chloe had wanted to talk to him, even before Meeree had urged her. More importantly, though, she wanted him to talk to her. Why couldn't he open up? What was blocking him? Perhaps if she told him how she felt, would that help? No. That would only make matters worse.

'So…Jalak's settled?' he asked, when the silence became unbearable. Part of him hadn't wanted Chloe to join him, preferring to be alone with his thoughts, but the other part—the part that was having a difficult time keeping his hands off her—wanted her a lot closer than she was now.

'Yes. Meeree will look after him.'

'They have an amazing relationship. It's nice to see.'

'I guess there are a lot of broken marriages nowadays.'

He nodded. 'I think I mentioned that my parents divorced.'

'Yes, you did.' Chloe's throat was suddenly dry but she asked her next question, knowing full well she was about to open a can of worms. 'Is that why you don't want to get married?'

'Because my parents' marriage didn't work? No.'

'Then why?'

He looked at her and rubbed his jaw with his finger and thumb, wondering how best to answer that. 'Why do you ask?'

'Because I want to know.'

'Why?'

'Because it's important to me.'

'Why?'

'Fair dinkum, Michael, don't you think I have a right to know? And why are you being so evasive?'

'Perhaps it's none of your business.'

'None of my…' She trailed off, shaking her head, totally exasperated with him. 'How dare you?'

'How dare I? You were the one who started with the prying questions.'

'I think I have a right to know,' she repeated. Meeree had told her not to be impatient but it was difficult when the man was making her crazy by trying to wind her around in circles.

'Why?'

'Because there's something real between us, Michael. We didn't ask for it but it's there. I just want to know why you're afraid of marriage. Why you think it is so wrong for you?'

'I'm not afraid of marriage. I've never once said that. I simply choose not to get married.'

'Why?' Her tone was imploring.

He stood and walked away from her, and for a moment she thought she might actually get an answer, but instead, when he turned to face her again, she could see in the torchlight that his face was a set mask.

He had to hurt her. He had to drive her away. It was for her own good as well as his. He loved her yet to tell her that, to confess what he felt so deep down inside, would only cause both of them anguish. Even if she didn't return his feelings in the same way, she was fixating on this marriage question and it was better to hurt her now rather than down the track. 'I don't really see what my reasons have to do with you. So we have an attraction. So we've shared a couple of kisses and confidences. That's the way of the world, Chloe. We meet people, we touch each other's lives and then we move on.'

'And you're moving on, right?'

'It's a non-issue,' he said with his palms held up. 'PMA will be picking us up the day after tomorrow. You'll be on your one month of forced leave and I'll be flying off somewhere else with PMA, probably by the end of the week.'

'So you're still going to do it?'

'What? Work with PMA? Sure. Why wouldn't I?'

Chloe stared at him. 'Well, it's not as though you're loving it out here.'

He shrugged. 'I don't *dislike* it, but it's not my life. I'm happy to help, to be a part of something bigger, but when my time's up I'm more than happy to return to my life in Sydney.'

And there she had it. He was city, she was country. He was new, she was old. He was shiny and she was dull.

'Fine. You've made your point. We have chemistry between us but nothing more.' She held her breath, hoping he'd contradict her, hoping he'd prove her wrong by confessing undying love for her, but he remained silent. 'There's just one thing I want to know and I want an honest answer.'

Again he was silent, waiting for her question.

'The truth, Michael. Why don't you want to marry?'

He looked down at the ground, his mind in a turmoil. He'd thought for a moment there that she'd been willing to just leave it at that. He should have known better. During the past few days he'd discovered she wasn't a woman to let the little things go, and while he'd appreciated her attention to detail, he didn't like it when it was directed at him.

Still, perhaps if he told her, she'd leave him alone and they could both start forgetting each other sooner rather than later.

He looked up and met her gaze. 'I have cancer, Chloe.'

'You're in remission,' she argued.

'It could come back at any time.'

'People have been cured of Hodgkin's lymphoma in the past.'

'Cured.' He scoffed at the word. 'Right.'

'What, so you're just going to go through life holding yourself aloof from relationships?'

'Hey, you of all people should understand. If you'd

known your husband had had cancer, would you have married him?'

Chloe shook her head and narrowed her gaze. 'Leave my life out of this.'

'Why? It's a perfect illustration. Look what you went through after his death. I can understand why he pulled away, Chloe, and let me just say it had nothing to do with you. Being faced with your own mortality isn't a fun thing to cope with.'

'I know.'

'You know? How? Have you had cancer?'

'No, you dolt,' she almost yelled, before remembering there were other people about who were probably trying to sleep. 'I almost died in a plane crash the other day.'

Both of them were silent, reality seeping in around them.

'Cancer doesn't hold all the cards when it comes to facing one's mortality or losing control over one's life. Well, let me tell you that you will *never* get control over your life. Things happen, Michael, things that you can't plan for, that you can't foresee. One minute you're heading home on a forced vacation and the next you're in a plane that is hurtling towards the ground at an alarming speed. Then there's mudslides and snakes, and people with guns and falling in love and trying to figure out just what on earth is happening! There is knowledge, there is wisdom and there is learning to be content with that and, hopefully, if you're very fortunate, that contentment will bring peace and happiness with it.'

He stared at her, wondering for a second whether he'd misheard or misunderstood what she'd just said. 'Falling in love?' he asked, his throat dry.

A dawning realisation crossed her face then she straightened her shoulders and flipped her hair. He groaned, positive she had no idea how incredible she looked when she did that. He'd seen her in all sorts of moods during the past few days, but he'd never seen her as strong and defiant as she was right now.

'Yes.'

'With me?'

'Yes.'

Michael's heart secretly rejoiced at the knowledge while his head immediately rejected it. 'Don't.'

'Too late.'

'I'll only hurt you, Chloe.'

'Because you won't marry me?'

'No. Because I'll *never* marry.'

'Because of the cancer.'

'Yes.'

'Then you're a coward.' She turned to go, to head into the hut, but he grabbed her arm and swung her round to face him, so surprising her with his quick move that he knocked her off balance. His hands gripped her upper arms, steadying her, and when she looked up into his face, she saw that he was angry—really angry.

'You think it's cowardice to protect a loved one from watching you die? You think it's cowardice to protect a child from dying?'

'This isn't about me,' she said softly.

'No. It's about me. My father gave me Hodgkin's, Chloe. He contracted it and I watched him die. Then I go in for routine testing and, wham, I find I have it, too. I carry the genes, genes that will be passed on to any children I might have.' His hold on her softened before he dropped his hands completely, as though he'd totally given up the fight. 'I've suffered enough and so have you. The last thing either of us needs is more pain. I won't let you watch me die and I won't even contemplate having children, running the risk of perhaps watching them die, knowing it was I who poisoned them in the first place. I refuse to do it, Chloe, and that's all there is to it.'

CHAPTER TEN

CHLOE refused to leave Tarparnii, contacting PMA to say she was still needed there because of a very sick baby and would return to Australia once her other colleagues returned from doing their clinics. There was no way she could be on the plane with Michael. It would just hurt too much.

He hadn't slept in their hut and had walked out with a few of the men the following day to take a look at the area surrounding the village, successfully avoiding her. That's the way it had stayed, the two of them having an uncomfortable few minutes together just before he'd left the village with West to head back to the airport.

They'd looked at each other, unsure whether to embrace or shake hands or simply nod politely. Finally, Michael had simply said, 'Take care, Chloe,' before walking down the track that led away from the village. He hadn't turned around, hadn't looked back. If he had, he would have seen the tears flowing down her cheeks.

She hadn't felt pain like this for years and now that she was older, more experienced with life, it only hurt more. True to her word, though, she stayed in the village to care for the baby, who was improving daily, and Jalak, who was up and about in no time at all.

'I am a fast healer,' Jalak told her after she'd changed his bandage. 'You are not.'

'No.' She didn't have to guess he wasn't talking about a physical injury where she was concerned.

'Keep going, Chloe. Always, you must keep going.' He tapped his head. 'This will guide you.' He pointed to his eyes. 'This will show you.' He tapped his chest, indicating his heart beneath. 'This will reap the reward.'

'Oh, Jalak,' she said and leant her head on his shoulder. 'What am I going to do?'

'Find your home, *Separ.*'

'I thought it was here.'

'No. This is a dwelling. You must find your home.'

Chloe lifted her head and kissed his cheek. 'Find my home,' she repeated, her eyes lit with unshed tears.

As she let herself into her apartment back in Sydney, she had no sense of coming home. The place was usually rented out and therefore had very few personal touches. She unlocked one small storeroom where she kept her clothes and things like books, photo albums and small treasures from her past.

When Craig and Nate had died, she'd boxed everything up and shoved it in a corner, and now she knew it was time to take it out, dust it off and face it head on. Three hours later she was surrounded by various memories and, instead of making her cry, most of them had made her smile. A picture of her wedding, a snapshot of Nate. His bootees, which now simply smelled of mothballs, rather than baby. She'd put her memories, her emotions into storage, instead of airing them and appreciating them.

'It's not too late,' she whispered to the paraphernalia around her. Was it too late for her and Michael? She hadn't heard from him and didn't expect to, but where he might think they were done, she knew they were only just beginning.

'Look out, mate,' she said as she stood. 'I'm coming to find my home.' She laughed as the weight seemed to roll off her shoulders. 'He isn't going to know what hit him.' First, though, she had some research to do.

Michael closed his eyes, trying to control his thoughts as the plane descended towards the runway. Sweat beaded his brow and he gripped the armrest tighter. He wasn't sure if his tension was due to the plane or the fact that in another second he'd be back in Tarparnii.

Was she there? She had to be there. She'd refused to leave and even if she had eventually left, it had been over a month since he'd last been there, which meant Chloe could have taken her enforced leave and then returned to the place she loved most.

He'd spent the last month working for PMA in Papua New Guinea and had appreciated the opportunity to work himself into an exhausted sleep every night. It had been long hours, lots of patients, and he'd welcomed the distraction from his thoughts…the thoughts that always seemed to be centred around Chloe.

Even when he'd slept, she'd been in his dreams. Sometimes he'd close his eyes and imagine he could smell her scent, feel her hair, touch her lips. The woman was a part of him, just like the blood pumping through his veins and the air passing through his lungs. He loved her with every breath he took and now…now there was a strong possibility he would see her again.

Initially he'd told PMA he hadn't wanted to return to Tarparnii but now, when a colleague had become ill in PNG, there was a vacancy and, if the truth was told, Michael *wanted* to see Chloe again.

He was headed for Meeree and Jalak's village and was pleased at the prospect of seeing them again, as well as friends like Bel and Belhara. He'd also been learning a bit of the language, his colleagues in PNG happy to tease and teach, and where he thought he'd never grasp it, he was slowly coming to understand more every day.

That wasn't the only thing he was coming to understand. His need for Chloe was intense and that was when he was apart from her. How was he going to control his thoughts and emotions when she was right in front of him? His love for her had only grown and whoever had said that absence made the heart grow fonder had certainly had him in mind where Chloe was concerned.

Finally, the wheels of the small plane touched *terra firma* and Michael opened his eyes, but his breathing didn't return to normal. No. It wasn't the plane that had his body in such an uproar, which only meant it was the thought of seeing Chloe again. Would they be able to work as colleagues? Would they be able to put what was between them aside? Could he be within two feet of her and not want to hold her, touch her, kiss her? He doubted it.

Did she still love him? He hoped so. Hoped that he hadn't pushed her away once and for all. To think she might have discarded him from her thoughts and moved on was something he found difficult to contemplate but, then, from what he knew of her, she wasn't the type of person to treat her emotions lightly. She'd mourned her husband and son for many years, trying to survive what had happened to her, and she had. She had strength, she had purpose and he loved every stubborn, strong-willed bone in her body.

As he exited the plane with two other PMA personnel, calling his thanks to the pilots, he headed over to where the transport was waiting for them. It would only take them so far and the rest of the journey they would have to complete on foot.

When they were dropped off and walking up the dirt path, Michael was surprised when Jalak seemed to appear out of nowhere, saying he'd come to meet them. He took Michael's hands in his in the traditional Tarparniian greeting before embracing him like a long-lost relative.

Michael smiled and spoke in Tarparnese, hoping he got it right. Jalak laughed and praised his attempts. 'You have been missed, Michael.'

'How is Meeree?' Michael asked.

'She is well.'

'And your shoulder?'

'As you see, it is fine.'

'Good.' Michael remained silent for a while, wondering how best to ask if Chloe was around. Was she in the village? Was she waiting for him? Did she even know he was coming? Did she want to see him? Perhaps she'd specifically asked to go to a different village? It also appeared Jalak wasn't going to be offering any information, so he had to content himself with looking at the scenery—not that he registered anything he saw.

The other people kept up the chatter and before he knew it Michael looked around, surprised to find they were already at the village, although this time it looked slightly different. People were everywhere; decorations were being hung from the trees and huts. A large mound of wood was in the centre of the grassed area. Food was being brought out and put on tables. Women were sitting, stringing flowers together into colourful leis. The entire place was a hub of activity.

'What's going on?' he asked, shifting his canvas bag.

'It is the *par'Mach*. It is a night to dance and remember the old ones.' Jalak was interrupted by his wife, who walked quickly across to squeeze Michael's hands before embracing him.

'We are so happy to welcome you back. Come.' Her gaze encompassed everyone. 'I will take you to your hut.'

As Michael followed, he kept searching the people, looking for Chloe. She shouldn't be that difficult to find with her fair skin and blonde hair. They were given the same hut as before, but this time there were sleeping mats in every corner of the one-room building.

'Find a space,' she said, then looked at Michael. 'I will need to see you.'

He nodded, his heartbeat intensifying at her words. Was Chloe all right? Was she sick? Was she here? The questions tumbled around in his mind but he forced himself to remain calm and followed Meeree outside.

'She is not here,' Meeree said, and Michael nodded, now quite used to the woman's insight. He couldn't believe how depressed he suddenly felt. All that anticipation and worry for nothing. Chloe wasn't here. He stopped walking, unsure he would ever move his legs again.

'Is she…?' He stopped and cleared his throat, amazed to find he felt like crumbling to the ground in a heap, never to get up again. 'Is she well?'

'Chloe? She is fine, Michael. You, though, do not look the best. You need good food.'

He needed more than that. He needed Chloe. While he'd been away from her it had been easier but now, now that he was back in the place where their love had begun, he couldn't bear to be separated from her. Yet he was.

'Food? Right.' He shook his head, the total loss of his true love swamping him. What had he done? How could he even have thought he could continue to breathe without her? She was such an intimate and integral part of his life, part of his heart. 'Meeree?'

She smiled her indulgent smile and placed her hand on his arm. 'You will be fine. The night will begin soon and the *par'Mach* is something not to miss.'

'I think I can do without it.'

'But I insist.'

Michael met her gaze and saw the urgency there. 'I will go, for you—but I won't stay long.'

Meeree inclined her head slightly. 'Many thanks. Now I must prepare. The sun is almost on the trees.' As she walked away, Michael watched as several people began lighting extra torches and not long after that the bonfire in the centre was lit. People were everywhere, laughing and smiling and having a fantastic time. Many couples were holding hands and stealing kisses. Love was definitely in the air…and it was the last thing he needed. It was as though they were purposely rubbing salt in the wound.

Michael turned away and went into the hut, glad it

was now vacant as everyone else was eager to be out and doing, being involved and helping. He had no such desire. All he wanted was to find Chloe. He'd been an absolute idiot to even think he could get over her. Now that he was back, back where it had all begun, he knew he wouldn't be able to leave until he found out where she was and what she was doing. It was selfish of him, wanting her to be with him when he couldn't promise her a life of happiness. The risk of his cancer returning was, admittedly, not high, but it was there nevertheless and although she'd already lost Craig to cancer, he simply couldn't live his life without her. He was a selfish man and he hated himself for not being stronger.

When the drums and music started, he stopped staring at the walls and went outside to fulfil his promise to Meeree. The instant he stepped outside, his jaw dropped at what he saw before him.

Chloe. There were torches burning brightly on either side of the steps leading to their hut, giving the impression of a halo of light around her. Was she real? Was he hallucinating?

She was smiling brightly at him…*his* Chloe. She was there and she was standing outside the hut wearing the most glorious white dress. It was made of a light fabric that flowed around her legs and arms, making her look like an angel floating towards him. He blinked and shook his head, trying to control his senses.

Slowly, she raised her hand and beckoned him to come closer. His legs moved and as they did he remembered to close his mouth, swallowing his disbelief at seeing her there. When he stood close, close enough to touch her, he reached out a hand, surprised when it trembled. His fingers sifted through her fine golden hair and he groaned, his control snapping.

He urged her head to his, their lips meeting in a powerful reunion, both of them hungry and eager for the other. He loved her. He loved this woman with the air in his lungs, with the blood in his veins, with the passion in his heart… And she loved him back.

So much had happened, but out of the darkness had come this spark of light, this spark of hope, this spark of love. As he deepened the kiss, she went with him, matching his need completely and holding nothing back. She needed to show him that she was serious, that her love for him was very real and not the work of a moment.

Her heart thudded wildly against her chest as his mouth continued to take her to new heights. She'd never realised a kiss could convey so much of a person's emotions…until she'd first kissed Michael. What was raging between them had been brewing since she'd first boarded the plane, slowly simmering away beneath the surface until this point in time. They were supposed to be together for the rest of their lives and she knew that was exactly what was going to happen, despite his objections. She was prepared to knock them all down when he voiced them. His fears, his concerns, she would cure each and every one because he belonged to her. She'd been given a second chance at happiness and she wasn't going to ignore that. Life was too short.

When his mouth broke from hers, both of them gasping for air, she was glad he'd stopped. The connection between them was so powerful, so intense, it zapped all her strength. Yet when Michael began trailing butterfly kisses down her throat, a new wave of fire sprang to life inside her body, renewing her energy. He kissed her collar-bone, along the neckline of her dress and back up the other side to nuzzle her ear. By the time he got there, she was trembling.

'Are you cold?' His voice was thick with repressed desire but his concern was touching.

She swallowed. 'No.' Lifting her head, she opened her eyes and looked at him, her love radiating out towards him. 'It's you, Michael.' Her words were a whisper filled with wonder. 'You make me like this.'

That stunned him. 'I do?'

She smiled. 'Yes. You make me feel cherished and special.'

'Wow.'

Her smile increased and he was totally captivated.

'Come.' She reached for his hands and together they walked towards the celebrations. 'The *par'Mach* festival. You don't want to miss it.'

'I don't care where I am, as long as I'm with you,' he said softly, and she stopped walking, turning to face him.

'Really?'

His gaze was imploring. 'Yes. I'm in love with you, Chloe.'

She'd known it, felt it, but to hear him say it took her breath away, and that was something that had never happened to her before. Her smile was bright and she knew that soon her cheeks would start to ache but she didn't care. She was so incredibly happy.

'This is perfect,' she finally said.

Michael tugged on her hand, wanting to draw her

closer, but apart from allowing him to press a brief yet hungry kiss on her lips she edged away.

'Don't spoil it,' she said with a laugh.

'Spoil what?'

'The *par'Mach*.'

They continued on their way to where the villagers from near and far were gathered. 'And what exactly is this *par'Mach*?'

'It translates to mean the festival of love.'

'Love?' He raised his eyebrows. 'Then that *is* appropriate.'

She laughed again and he loved to hear it, loved to watch her face light up, free of stress and worry. She was so incredibly beautiful…and she loved him. 'It is a very special day in the Tarparniian calendar. Many *par'-machkai* wait for this day to publicly announce their love in a binding ceremony.'

'Binding?'

'Marriage.'

Michael gaped, his sluggish brain slowly catching up. 'Marriage?' he asked, as though he hadn't heard her correctly.

She laughed. 'Relax. I'm not about to drag you to the altar. This isn't about us.'

They began to mingle with the villagers, their hands firmly joined. Now that they'd found each other again, neither seemed ready to let go. 'Where were you earlier?' he asked. 'When I arrived, Meeree told me you weren't here.'

Chloe laughed. 'She was probably teasing you. I wasn't in the village itself. I was out at the waterhole with other women, helping with the preparations.'

Michael joined in her laughter. 'Well, I'll forgive Meeree this time, but only because you look so utterly beautiful.'

She smiled shyly at him. 'I do?'

'How can you have any doubt?' He cupped her cheek in his hand, his thumb caressing her lips. 'You're exquisite.'

A loud bang made them all jump and Michael looked around, concerned. 'What was that?'

Chloe smiled at him. 'It signals the beginning of the festival.' A cheer went up, proving her point, and Michael leaned down to say something, his breath fanning down her neck, giving her goose bumps.

'How can they have this festival? The country is full of unrest.'

'It is *the* festival. There will always be unrest and upheaval in this world, either here or elsewhere. It's the way of the world, Michael, but what this festival does is give people the chance to remember the time of peace and that their country is indeed worth fighting for. If we all stayed inside and cowered under the beds when things became rough, well…we'd all waste away to nothing.'

She looked up at him with an adoring gaze. 'That was how I was until you found me. I'd locked myself away, intent on merely surviving. If it wasn't for you, I'd still be hiding under the bed, afraid to see what life was all about, to take a chance once more. You rescued me, Michael.'

He pressed a kiss to her lips before nodding, realising in that instant that although he'd told her he loved her, he was still hiding. 'You shame me, Chloe.'

'How?'

'With your strength, your trust and your love. You are

willing to put yourself out there, and while I want to, I don't know if I can.'

'Because you love me?'

'Yes.' How could she possibly understand? It was strange but she did. 'I love you so much that I don't want to put you through any more pain and anguish…yet still I want you. I want you by my side, with me in everything I do for the rest of my life, and as I have no idea how long that will be, it's an extremely selfish request.'

'None of us knows how long our lives will be, Michael. You've helped me to step outside my comfort zone, to take a chance on life again, to experience new and exciting things that I more than likely won't have any control over, but with you by my side I feel as though I can accomplish anything. You say I have strength and trust and love? That's because you inspire them in me.'

Chloe smiled up at him. 'I went back to Australia for my month's leave and I faced my past. I looked at photographs, watched old movies and relived the good times, but I also realised I'd changed so much since then. I'm a different person to who I was back then, and you know what?'

He raised his eyebrows questioningly, overcome by the light that lit her from the inside.

'I like me.'

Michael placed his hands on her shoulders and edged her closer. 'I'm glad. I like you, too. A lot!'

Chloe giggled, feeling young and free and pretty and loved. She accepted his kisses, feeling they were almost there. Almost at the point where they could both be truly happy. He had a few more steps to take but at least tonight he was willing to do that.

'Ah, Chloe,' he said, lifting his head. 'I love you, I honestly do. When I'm with you my life is…perfect. What I feel for you…it's powerful and wild and I can't believe the extent of the emotions you evoke in me. I want them. I need them—all of them—and I need them for ever but…what if I get sick again?'

'And what if you don't?'

'All right. What if I don't? We can't ever have children.'

'Why not?'

He looked down at her, immediately exasperated. 'You *know* why not.'

'Because you might pass on the genes. Yes, you've said that once before.'

'You don't think that's important?'

'Of course I do, and you were wise to be concerned, but did you have all the facts?'

'Facts?'

'The statistics on Hodgkin's lymphoma. It's not conclusive that it's a hereditary disease, Michael.'

'I don't care about the stats, Chloe. My father had it. I had it.'

She shrugged. 'Un-luck of the draw. Craig had cancer twice. Both were completely unrelated. These things happen. You may pass on genes and you may not. The point is, we would be prepared. With you, they discovered your cancer early, they were able to treat it and you could quite easily never be touched by it again. Yes, it's a chance and, yes, it means giving up the tight control you want to have over your life but you can't. Control is a myth, Michael. Trying to find it is like looking for a needle in a haystack. Living life, taking chances—albeit not reckless ones—is a way of finding yourself, of growing, of not hiding under the bed, afraid to accept change. Living life also provides its own rewards. Honesty, love and wisdom are just a few.'

'You're starting to sound like Meeree.'

Chloe smiled. 'I take that as a big compliment.'

'I've heard everything you've said,' he began. 'And I agree with it.' He paused and shook his head. 'It's just difficult to take that first step.'

She gripped both his hands in hers. 'You're not alone, Michael. I'm already out on that limb, I've taken the step of faith and put myself out there, and I want to be out there with you. Thanks to you, I've found I no longer need to stay in Tarparnii to find happiness. Jalak told me to find my home—so I went back to Sydney.' Chloe shrugged. 'It wasn't there. It's not here in the village.' She met his gaze, love lighting her brown eyes. 'It's with you, Michael. You are my home and I want to stay with you for ever. Trust me, my darling. Let me be there for you just as you are there for me. Whatever our future holds— let's discover it together. The good and the bad. We can do it, we can accept and we can fight when necessary.'

Michael knew everything she said was the truth. The statistics regarding Hodgkin's lymphoma were true and it was highly possible he hadn't contracted the disease from his father. Perhaps it had just been 'un-luck', as Chloe had called it.

He also knew he'd used his past, the cancer, as an excuse. He'd been hurt by his father's death, by what had happened to him, and separating himself from the rest of the world, living in his own bubble, had helped him to cope with what had happened. Now, though, he didn't need to cope any more. He could trust and love and he knew Chloe would never let him down.

'What does *par'machkai* mean?'

Chloe was surprised by his question. 'Uh…it means romantic partner for life.'

'And this *par'Mach* thing is like a wedding?'

'Yes. We've covered that.'

He looked out to where couples were dancing slowly around the bonfire, family and friends cheering them on and joining in the celebration of the shared love. When his gaze returned to Chloe, he had no more doubts.

'Well,' he drawled, taking a small step backwards, 'I'm not sure what the official Tarparniian custom is but…' He went down on one knee, holding her hands firmly with his own. 'Be my *par'machkai,* Chloe. Be my romantic partner for life. Please?'

It was her turn to gape at him, her mouth open in astonishment. Happiness swelled within her and tears glistened in her eyes. Closing her mouth, she tried to speak but found he'd once more taken her breath away. This man, this wonderful, special man who had also had so much hurt in his life. They were so perfect for each other, both needing and giving help, both loving and trusting so strongly, even though they sometimes drove each other crazy. She smiled down at him, still unable to believe he wanted to be with her—for ever.

'Chloe? I want to marry you,' he clarified. 'Not only here in Tarparnii but back home in Australia. I want you with me for ever.'

'I want that, too. So *very* much.' She tugged on his hands and he came to stand beside her.

'Is that a yes?'

She laughed, unable to believe she could feel this happy. 'Yes. Of course it's a yes.' Her mouth met his in a promise, a promise that they would be together for ever.

'Do we get to dance out there now?' he asked, when they finally were able to part.

'Yes.'

Together they walked out and a cheer went up from the crowd. Beneath the moon and starry sky, they promised their love to each other, their hands bound together.

'I love you, Chloe.'

'I love you, too,' she whispered back, as their lips eagerly met once more.

'This feels so…perfect,' he murmured against her mouth. 'You're so perfect.'

'Mr and Mrs Perfectly Happy.' She glanced away for a moment and gasped as she saw a star shoot its way across the indigo sky.

'Make a wish,' Michael whispered.

'I don't need to.' She smiled at him with all the love in her heart. 'I already have everything I could ever want.'

EPILOGUE

MICHAEL SAT IN HIS office, finishing off sorting through his in-tray. Time was getting on and he wanted this work done so he could concentrate on his very important date tonight. The phone rang and, frowning, he snatched it up.

'Dr Hill,' he said into the receiver.

'Dr Hill, this is A and E. We have an emergency.'

Michael was about to growl into the phone that they must call someone else when the sweet, feminine tone from Sydney General's top A and E specialist penetrated his preoccupation with his paperwork. He breathed in and settled back in his chair, tossing his pen onto the desk. 'Really? What's the situation?'

'A female patient has presented with wild heart palpitations and a strange growling noise coming from her stomach.'

'Sounds as though she needs to see a cardiologist.'

'I beg to differ. She needs the touch of a very *special* specialist. One with your *exact* qualifications. The situation is quite serious, Doctor. She may even require mouth-to-mouth resuscitation.'

Michael grinned, loving the way Chloe teased him. 'Sounds intriguing. Thank you for bringing this patient to my attention. Is she mobile? Is she able to walk?'

'Yes.'

'Good. Have her ready for me. I'll be down in five minutes.'

'Five minutes?' The sweet tone on the other end of the phone changed to one of impatience.

'Two minutes,' he amended as he stood and grabbed his jacket.

'Two minutes?'

'Fine. I'm walking out the door now.' He put the phone down and raced out of his office, flicking off the light switch and locking the door as he left. It took him less than a minute to go down the stairs to the A and E department, and when he arrived there, the A and E specialist was standing with her hands in her hips, tapping her foot.

'What took you so long?' she said with a grin, her arms immediately going around his neck.

'Sorry.. There were a few things I needed to tie up, especially as we'll be away in Tarparnii for the next three months.' Michael kissed the specialist passionately. The staff around them simply ignored them. They were used to this sort of behaviour from their general surgeon and his wife.

'Ready to go?' he asked.

'Yes.' Chloe turned and waved goodbye to her A and E staff. 'See you all in a few months' time,' she said.

'Right,' Michael said as they walked towards the door. 'Next on the agenda, I'm going to take my wife out for dinner. I've been told by a very reliable source that her stomach has been growling.'

As they walked to the car, Chloe snuggled close to her husband. 'I can't believe it's one year today since we had our binding ceremony.'

'Time flies when you're having fun.'

'Want to have more fun?' she asked, as he opened the car door for her.

He grinned, lifting one eyebrow in delight. 'What do you have in mind?'

She shrugged. 'How about parenthood?'

Michael froze.

'Darling, are you OK?'

'What? How? When?'

She laughed again and kissed him. 'A baby,' she said, answering his questions. 'And I think you know *how* and in about eight months' time.'

Michael's stunned look turned to one of panic and Chloe placed a hand on his cheek. Instantly, he let go of his worries and smiled. He trusted the woman before him and one year ago she'd made a promise to always love him and to always be there for him.

'I'm going to be a father?'

'Yep.' Chloe leaned over and placed a kiss on his lips. 'You most certainly are.'

'How do you know? Have you seen anyone?'

'Not yet. We'll do that together.'

'Have you been sick?'

'Nope. I'm only a few days late but I had a hunch so I did a test just before I called you.'

'And it was positive.'

'It was.'

'But we leave in three days to go back to Tarparnii.'

'Which gives us enough time to see a specialist and

make sure everything is fine. It'll be fine, Michael.' Her words reassured him. 'Meeree and Jalak are going to be so happy.'

Michael placed a hand on his wife's flat belly, knowing he was going to love watching her grow round and radiant with his child. 'You're amazing,' he whispered. 'You have such strength, such confidence, such love.'

'I get it from you,' she said, and kissed him. 'I love you, Michael.'

He smiled down at his beautiful, pregnant wife. 'I love you too, *Separ.*'

0107/03a

MILLS & BOON®

Live the emotion

_Medical
romance™

A WIFE AND CHILD TO CHERISH
by Caroline Anderson

The Audley's new consultant, Patrick Corrigan,
is overawed by nurse and single mum Annie
Mortimer's courage and fierce independence.
Annie and her daughter bring out Patrick's
protective instincts – being near them gives him a
purpose that he thought he would never feel again.
But can Patrick convince Annie that his love is
unconditional…?

THE SURGEON'S FAMILY MIRACLE
by Marion Lennox

When surgeon Ben Blayden arrives on the exotic
island of Kapua he is stunned to find that the island's
doctor is Lily Cyprano, the girl he loved at medical
school…and that she has a seven year old son – his
son – Benjy! Ben has always avoided emotional ties,
but will Lily and the charm of his new-found son give
him the courage to claim the loving family he needs?

A FAMILY TO COME HOME TO
by Josie Metcalfe

Single mother Dr Kat Leeman is relieved to hire
a temporary GP – and single father Ben Rossiter
is perfect for the job. Ben and his daughter never
settle anywhere for long, but something about Kat
makes him want to stay. If Ben can face his past and
heal Kat's heart they may both have a very special
family to come home to…

On sale 2nd February 2007

*Available at WHSmith, Tesco, ASDA,
and all good bookshops*

www.millsandboon.co.uk

THE LONDON CONSULTANT'S RESCUE
by Joanna Neil

Dr Emma Granger enjoys rescuing people all over London with the air ambulance team. Her boss, Rhys Benton, is professional, caring and fully in control – everything a consultant should be. Emma believes that he could never see her as anything more than a colleague, but when Emma's life is in danger, Rhys has the opportunity to show her how he really feels.

THE DOCTOR'S BABY SURPRISE
by Gill Sanderson

Gorgeous doctor Toby Sinclair has a reputation as a carefree playboy. But when his baby son – who he never knew existed – lands on his doorstep, Dr Annie Arnold can't refuse Toby's plea for help. And as Annie watches Toby bonding with his baby, she wonders if they might just have a future together after all…

THE SPANISH DOCTOR'S CONVENIENT
BRIDE **by Meredith Webber**

Obstetrician Marty Cox cannot help growing attached to the baby girl in NICU, but she knows that the father – when they find him – will want to take his child away. The attraction between Marty and Dr Carlos Quintero is instant and, realising how devoted Marty is to his daughter, Carlos proposes a marriage of convenience.

On sale 2nd February 2007

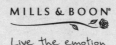

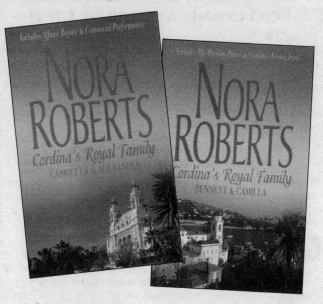

4 FREE

BOOKS AND A SURPRISE GIFT!

We would like to take this opportunity to thank you for reading this Mills & Boon® book by offering you the chance to take FOUR more specially selected titles from the Medical Romance™ series absolutely FREE! We're also making this offer to introduce you to the benefits of the Mills & Boon® Reader Service™—

- ★ **FREE home delivery**
- ★ **FREE gifts and competitions**
- ★ **FREE monthly Newsletter**
- ★ **Exclusive Reader Service offers**
- ★ **Books available before they're in the shops**

Accepting these FREE books and gift places you under no obligation to buy, you may cancel at any time, even after receiving your free shipment. Simply complete your details below and return the entire page to the address below. You don't even need a stamp!

YES! Please send me 4 free Medical Romance books and a surprise gift. I understand that unless you hear from me, I will receive 6 superb new titles every month for just £2.80 each, postage and packing free. I am under no obligation to purchase any books and may cancel my subscription at any time. The free books and gift will be mine to keep in any case.

M7ZED

Ms/Mrs/Miss/Mr .... Initials ....

BLOCK CAPITALS PLEASE

Surname ....

Address ....

....

.... Postcode ....

Send this whole page to:
UK: FREEPOST CN81, Croydon, CR9 3WZ